KING ARTHUR'S DAUGHTER
Vera Chapman

AVON
PUBLISHERS OF BARD, CAMELOT AND DISCUS BOOKS

This book forms part of the Arthurian trilogy
The Three Damosels. The *two* other volumes are
The Green Knight and *The King's Damosel*.

AVON BOOKS
A division of
The Hearst Corporation
959 Eighth Avenue
New York, New York 10019

Copyright © 1976 by Rex Collings Ltd.
Library of Congress Catalog Card Number: 78-58405
ISBN: 0-380-01958-2
Published by arrangement with Rex Collings Ltd.

First Avon Printing, June, 1978

KNIGHTHOOD

Sir Bedivere—pledged to restore Arthur's true heir, this last loyal veteran wins to his cause the undying allegiance of . . .

Sir Ambrosius—the gallant knight who stood by the side of Ursulet, Arthur's only legitimate daughter, through raging conflict and breathless escape so they could raise children and preserve the Arthurian bloodline.

VILLAINY

Morgan le Fay—jubilant when Arthur's doom is sealed, she plots to usurp his lawful heir and crown her sinister puppet . . .

Mordred—who posed a deadly peril to Ursulet and plunged the realm into civil war, only to be swept aside by hordes of invading Saxons as Britain becomes England!

LEGEND!

Arthur—after the last great battle had been fought, and the Round Table disbanded, Arthur departed . . . . To die? Or to live in the spirit and blood of future generations of Englishmen?

◇◆◇

KING ARTHUR'S DAUGHTER is based on the engaging premise that Arthur fathered a daughter, Ursulet, and brings to a resounding conclusion Vera Chapman's brilliantly evocative trilogy of courtly life.

"Her beautiful, bejewelled prose runs with easy clarity, the strength and magic of her tale glinting with a subtle vein of humour." *London Daily Telegraph*

Contents

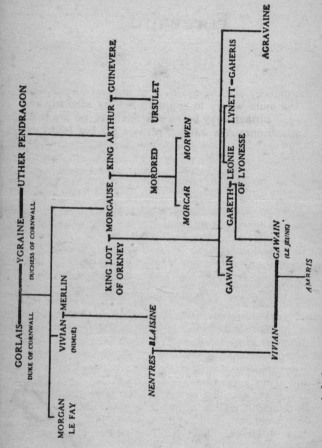

Author's note: Those in italics are my own invention. The rest are according to Malory.

Foreword

The chronology of King Arthur is at the foot of the rainbow. The more we try to approach him by scholarly research, the further away he recedes. He was, we are told, perhaps a Bronze Age warrior; perhaps the last leader of the Romano-British resistance against the Saxons; perhaps an old god of the British, or the eidolon, ikon or egregore of the British people and land, later projected as Saint George. Or perhaps he never existed at all, but was a pious invention of such writers as Geoffrey of Monmouth and Gerald of Wales, to fill a political need.

Yet there were ages when he was devoutly believed in; generation after generation has built up the shining figure, and from Malory onwards he, and all his company and environment, have become as solid and detailed as our admired Professor Tolkien's "Middle Earth." Milton considered "The Matter of Britain" as a serious subject; Tennyson and many others, culminating in the late T. H. White, have made Arthur and his Round Table more real to us than much of history. But no one can say, of course, what is or is not "true" about Arthur. The old romancers took the story as free for all, to retell it, elaborate it, or add to it. I have therefore ventured to do no more than any jongleur would have done.

Nobody can say that Arthur did *not* have a daughter. Kings' daughters, unless they make dynastic marriages, are apt to slip out of history and be ignored. So I present my invention of Ursulet, daughter of Arthur and Guinevere— Ursa Minor.

As to period. I have followed Malroy's lead, with something from Geoffrey of Monmouth; that is, a civilization more or less that of the twelfth century (with pardonable overtones from the fourteenth) but with the political situation as about the sixth century—the Romans not long

7

gone, the Jutes and Angles settled here and there, the old Celtic kingdom broken up and struggling for survival, and the Saxons about to descend in an avalanche.

So I present my tale, with no more pretensions to historical accuracy than were made by that good knight Sir Thomas Malory, on whose soul be peace.

ONE

✤

The Heiress and the Witch

THE stars of the summer night, with the Great Bear, constellation of Arthur, conspicuous among them, shone down on the walls and battlements of Camelot, and into the great hall where King Arthur sat lonely upon his dais.

There were two winding staircases in the extreme corners of the hall, and a screen masked the entrances to both. One led up to Arthur's own chamber, and the other to the Queen's. In the stillness, he could hear footsteps going up one of the stairways. Lancelot, going up to Guinevere's room. Well, let him go, then.

Pain squeezed Arthur's heart. That it should come to this! Lancelot, his friend, and Guinevere, his beloved. But he would not break in upon them. Better to swallow his bitter jealousy, and hide his humiliation, as long as he could—as long as Mordred would let him.

Mordred! That coarse-grained, swaggering youth, with the loud mouth and the dirty mind—his bastard son by the woman Morgause, the Queen of Orkney, his own half-sister. Why, oh God, why had he ever let her have her way with him? It *must* have been enchantment—and God wot, he hadn't known at the time that she was his half-sister. Why should he be punished with a son like that? Never, oh never let the rule of Britain fall into Mordred's hands. Mordred's only care for any people he ruled would be to get all he could out of them for his own pleasures, to oppress and persecute them so that he could enjoy the sense of power. He, Arthur, "the Bear of Britain," had built up and unified his country in the face of the encroaching barbarians; churches and monasteries and the arts of peace had flourished under him; the common men had lived in safety and happiness; and his chosen knights had learnt to aspire to such holiness as to reach out to the Holy Grail.

But Mordred would ruin all this. Mordred, if it suited his plan, would let the heathen in. Even now, he knew, Mordred was only waiting to force his hand about Guinevere, and precipitate the break-up of the kingdom in scandal and faction and civil war. Rather than that, he would shut his ears, for many nights yet, to those footsteps going up to Guinevere's room.

If only he and Guinevere had had a son—but there was only their little daughter—his beloved little daughter Ursulet, his "little bear," with her hair as white as Guinevere's. A woman could not rule in her own right—or could she? Some of the older races of the land held that the true inheritance was through the mother, not the father—and even that he himself held their allegiance by right of marrying Guinevere, the descendant of a long line of queens.

He roused himself. "Bedivere!"

"My lord?" He was not quite alone in the great hall; Sir Bedivere, who seldom was far from him in these days, had been sitting quietly beside the fire.

"Bedivere, is my scribe there?"

Bedivere called quietly for the scribe, a monk, who came with deep obeisance and stood ready to write.

"Good scribe, I want you to write this, and to have seven copies made, and send six to Chester, York, Winchester, London, Lincoln and Canterbury. Thus: I, Arthur, King of the Britons, do desire that at my death the crown shall pass to the Lady Ursulet, who is my lawful issue by Guinevere my Queen, and let no man deny this. Mordred my natural son is unlawfully born, being the son of Morgause, the Queen of Orkney, she being my mother's daughter. Let him not succeed to the throne of Britain, nor any of his issue. Let him be an Earl, and hold the feof of Maiden Castle in Dorset, but let him after my death hold the same in homage to Ursulet my aforementioned daughter, or else depart this realm. And let all men know, that though I die, *I shall come again*—Write that last in large letters, scribe: I SHALL COME AGAIN!"

The scribe carefully wrote the words down.

"Now have copies made," said Arthur, "and when all are made, bring me wax and my great seal, and I will seal them. You, Bedivere, shall keep the chief copy."

In one of the bedchambers of the castle, Mordred lay tossing on his bed, biting his nails, eaten up with desire. Not desire for any woman—he could have such as he desired easily enough—but worse, far worse. Desire for a crown and a throne. Desire for wealth. Desire for power. Desire for the name of a King.

So great was the power of his passion that it hung in the air around him like a cloud. It bristled and crackled with sudden spurts of hatred and cruelty. It reached out claws. And it called, called, called across the darkness for such powers as were of like kind with itself. Impossible that something should not hear and answer.

Out across marshes and plains, white vapours streaming from below the ground sent up a spurt of more solid vapour, that hovered, took direction, and sailed across the sky, like smoke drawn by the draught of a chimney. In the white cloud of vapour was something that laughed to itself, exulted in its own freedom and sense of power, rejoiced to break free from the earth where it had been hidden, and to feel its substance hardening again into the fine shapely limbs of a woman. The draught that had pulled it up from the ground pulled it straight towards the narrow window of Mordred's room, and inside.

He had not been quite asleep, but he jumped into full wakefulness to see a tall, pale, handsome lady, with jet-black hair and cat-like eyes, standing by his bedside.

"Who are you?" he exclaimed. "I don't remember having sent for you."

"You didn't." She smiled, a cold and rather eerie smile. "I'm not for your bed, my lad. I'm your aunt."

"My aunt?"

"Yes, your mother's sister. Morgause, Nimuë and I were three sisters, and Arthur was our brother. You know? Then you know that I am Morgan le Fay."

"My aunt Morgan—but they told me you were dead."

"Such as I don't die so easily. Now, now, my lad, no ceremony of welcome. I know what you want, and maybe I want the same. Oh yes, it was the power of your desire that drew me here. You want many things, but one thing more than all—you want to be King."

"Oh, I do, dear lady, I do."

"Why then, we may work together, I believe. But are you prepared to swear allegiance to me?"

"By all means, if you'll give me what I desire. I'll swear anything to any man—"

"I know you will," said she, again smiling coldly, "and

be forsworn again as readily. But this oath you will not forswear. Look in my eyes and you will see why you dare not."

And he looked in her eyes and knew.

So, trembling (although he was a bold man), he placed his hands between hers, and repeated,

"I, Mordred, swear to thee, Morgan le Fay, to be your liege man in word and deed, to my life's end and in the world to come."

Then she kissed him on his forehead, and it was like a red-hot coal.

"You will hear from me," she said, and went quietly out through the door, walking on golden sandals with her white robe swirling round her feet.

In another castle, miles away, a four-year-old boy whose name was Ambris started up from his sleep and screamed, "The Princess! The Princess! Save her! Save her!"

His mother stood beside him, tall and white in the dark, with her red hair over her shoulders.

"Hush, my love—no, wake up, there's nothing to be afraid of." She gathered him into her arms, and by degrees his terror subsided, he stopped trembling, and opened his eyes.

"You were dreaming, my dear. There now, it's gone."

He drew a long breath, looking up at her. "But I saw it," he said. "A battle, and there's the Princess. I had to save her."

His mother made the sign of the Cross over him. "So you shall in due time, my little one," she said. "So you shall. But go to sleep now."

After a minute's thought, she traced a pentagram in the air round him, the point upwards; and seeing that he was quiet now, she tiptoed away.

Her aunt-in-law, the stiff-backed, leather-faced Lynett, met her in the stony corridor.

"That child knows too much," she said.

Playing in the sunshine around the castle grounds, Ambris soon forgot the terrors of the night. It was a very pleasant castle, in seagirt Lyonesse—the south wall had a grassy slope outside, where his mother's little garden stood, full of flowers. The castle gates were never shut by day, for there were no enemies here in Lyonesse—no matter what might be in other parts of the world not so happy. King Arthur had put down the robbers, and kept the heathen Angles and Saxons at a distance. The grand glittering knights of Arthur's court, of whom Ambris was born to be one, rode to and fro about the country, redressing all wrongs. His father, Gawain the Younger, was one of these, and so were his grandfather Gareth and his great-uncles Gawain the Elder, Gaheris and Agravaine. They all rode out on adventures by the King's command, but Gawain his father was very often at home, with his mother Vivian, and his grandmother, the proud and dainty Leonie of Lyonesse, and his great-aunt, the tough old eccentric Lynett.

But the next night the dream came again, though differently.

He was standing by her bedside, where a small taper, like his own, gave a soft light; she was asleep and he could not see her face clearly, but she seemed only a little older than he was. A tall dark-haired woman came into the room, and opened a little box; and from the box a spider crawled out, such as he had never seen—huge, as big as a man's hand, black and hairy. The woman let it drop on the floor, and it crawled towards the Princess's bed.

It crawled rapidly, leg by horrible leg, over the rushes and the skin rug at the side of the bed, up the bedhanging towards the sleeping child. A black cat crouched by the child's pillow, as if to protect her, but though its green eyes were fixed on the crawling spider, and its hair was stiff on its back, it seemed powerless to move. Ambris could not move either. He tried to cry out a warning, to rush forward, but his body would not answer him. Then his terror for the helpless Princess, and his determination to save her, broke through whatever it was that held him, and he thrust out his hand with a huge effort, and pushed one of the tall unlit candlesticks that stood by the bed—it fell, missing the spider, but shaking it down on the floor—in the same instant the cat, as if released, sprang and crunched the spider's horny back in its teeth. He heard the cat's hoarse snarl as the dream broke, and he found himself awake in his own bed, sweating with remembered terror. But this time he did not cry out.

In Camelot at that same hour, Guinevere started up in bed, in her lover's arms. He too started.

13

"What was that? I heard a noise—"

"It's the turret room above—shall I go?"

"No, no—"

"Who sleeps above?"

"Ursulet and her nurse. It was the cat I heard. The cat guards her. If the nurse wakes she might come in here. Keep quiet—No, stay here, and I'll go." The very white lady slipped softly out of bed and threw a robe round her; so, carefully closing the door behind her, she went up the winding stair to the next room of the turret.

All was quiet and safe; Ursulet, her little daughter, slept undisturbed, only one of the great candlesticks had fallen over and in the corner the black cat was devouring something. Guinevere looked at her sleeping child—Arthur's "little bear"—and for a moment her heart misgave her. She had such a look of Arthur as she slept. Poor Arthur. . . . The white lady stooped and kissed the child's soft cheek. Then she went back to Lancelot.

"All's well," she said. "Black Gib caught a mouse, I think."

TWO

❧❦

The Convent

"URSULET," said the novice mistress, "Ursulet, you're dreaming. Get on with your work."

Ursulet, fourteen years old, gave a sigh, and picked up her needlework. She had indeed been dreaming. There was little else for her busy mind to do, now that most of her friends had left the convent. They had left, it was said, because the country was disturbed; but more than that she did not understand. There had been more than a dozen of them once; now there was only herself and Jeanne. So she had little company but dreams, and her dreams were mostly sad ones.

No sooner had she picked up the tambour frame and rethreaded her needle, however, than another nun came across the smooth lawns of the cloister garden.

"Ursulet, you're to go to the Lady Abbess at once."

She rose, as she had been taught to do, promptly but without unseemly haste, folded and put away her work, and went through the cloister arches and up the stone stairs with even step and downcast eye—but her heart was hammering. Being summoned to the presence of the Lady Abbess was always momentous, and sometimes frightening. She remembered the last time—when she had been called in to meet a tall grey man in a monk's habit, who yet didn't look like a monk—a man so thin, so wasted, she had never seen such a thin man, like a walking skeleton inside the sagging grey robe, with his hair and his beard like thistledown—she could not think that this had been Sir Lancelot, the gay gallant who used to be always with her mother. Very gently, with his big blue eyes running over with tears, he had told her that her mother was dead; and he had held her in his arms—his body, as she felt it through the threadbare habit, was almost nothing, a bundle of frail sticks—and they had cried together. Then the novice mistress had led her away dazed with shock, and as she went down the corridor she could still hear him sobbing in the room behind her.

So now she entered the same room full of apprehension. But there was no one with the Lady Abbess this time.

"Sit down, my child."

Ursulet, having curtsied, sat down on a low stool, with her back very straight and her hands folded. She was a very quiet little girl, for events had left their mark on her. She had long hair almost as lint-white as her mother's, who had been called "The White Apparition." But her eyes were like her father's, grey and with boldly marked brows.

"Yes, Reverend Mother?"

"You are fourteen years old. It is time that we thought of your future."

"Yes, Reverend Mother."

"You should consider preparing to take the vows."

Ursulet lifted her eyes for a moment.

"Reverend Mother—I am not sure that I have the vocation—that is—I am almost sure I have not."

The Abbess clicked her tongue.

"Child—I think you do not understand your position. You would no doubt think of a life in the world—of marriage?"

Ursulet dropped her eyes again. There were so many thoughts in her mind—to be sought in marriage, to have a lover—of course she had thoughts. Not to be all her life among old beldames!

She and her friends—while there were still a dozen girls like herself in the convent—had talked, and played the usual fortune-telling games. Last St. Agnes Eve they had gone through the whole ritual, pinning bay leaves to the corners of each one's pillow, and all had had dreams of one kind and another. But Jeanne had woken up screaming with the horrors, saying she was being devoured by a great horrible bear. They had laughed at her, and made jokes about Ursulet being the only little bear there—but Jeanne said it wasn't funny. It was horrible—something like a bear but worse—and then the novice mistress had heard the noise and come in, and given them all penance for taking part in heathenish practices. But Ursulet's own dream? Ah, that was something she told nobody.

She spoke now, with her eyes on her folded hands.

"Reverend Mother, I think my disposition might be towards being a wife in due time."

"Yes, my dear child. But be wise, and consider. These are ill times we live in, and who is to make a marriage for you? There is no peace and no safety in the country now. Do you know who you are?"

As if repeating a lesson, she replied, "I am the Princess Ursulet, only daughter of Authur the King and his Queen Guinevere."

"Even so, child. And being so, you stand in great danger." She turned back to the polished table that stood behind her, where were a chessboard and pieces. "Look, you know the game." She held up a delicate ivory pawn. "You are this pawn. There is only one left on the board, and if it can be moved up to the last square—here—it becomes a Queen. You understand? Many dangers lie in wait for that pawn.

"Your father's kingdom is gone, divided, broken—the Saxons overrun it, and warring factions split it up—there are many who will try to seize Arthur's daughter, to make good a claim to Arthur's throne. There were many in days of old, and there are still some, who consider that the lawful royal descent is from mother to daughter, not from father to son—the king reigns by right of marriage to the queen or the queen's daughter, as Arthur made good his claim to the Round Table by his marriage to Guinevere. There is one now, who I know would lay hands on you alive or dead. His name is Mordred. You know?"

Ursulet nodded.

"Arthur's son, but not lawful. I know he would try to have you for his own, to make good his claim to the kingdom."

Ursulet shuddered and her face crimsoned.

"But—my half-brother!"

"He would not care for that. He is a wicked man, and knows no law but his own will. If he could not get you with your consent, I think he would bring you to dishonour, so that your claim to the throne could no longer stand. He is capable of any villainy. So far, we have kept you hidden from him, but I do not know how long we can do so. Therefore, for your own safety, it were better that you should take the veil."

"But if he is so wicked and determined, Reverend Mother, would the veil be any protection?"

"We are in God's hands, child. Perhaps he would not respect even the veil—but it would be some barrier, some safeguard. It would be easier to hide you, or even to deny you if he traced you. Your name, your dangerous name and your lineage, would be forgotten, and you could serve God, live a quiet life here, and end your days in peace, safe from wicked and cruel men." The Abbess's calm smooth face was moved with emotion, and Ursulet almost saw tears in the fine hazel eyes. "Think of it, child, think of it."

"I will indeed think of it, Reverend Mother, but I cannot decide now."

"Of course not. Nothing can be decided hastily. Go now, dear child—fear nothing, but consider carefully what I have said."

She spoke a blessing over her and dismissed her. When the girl had gone, she sounded her small silver bell. A nun answered it.

"Sister Mary Salome, the situation is serious, they say. How near have the Saxons come?"

"As near as Poole, Reverend Mother."

"I had not thought them so near. Did the messenger reach Camelot?"

"He did, Reverend Mother, but the only answer was that they would send knights if they had any to spare—they did not say, *when* they had any to spare, but only *if*. I fear they will not come."

"Then we must do what we can in the time we have left. Call in the house-carles and all the men from the farms— such as there are. Set them to pile up logs against the doors and windows. Put the treasures in the hiding-place prepared for them." She sighed. "I am concerned for the young pupils. What can we do for them? There is nowhere we can send them in the time. They will be no safer anywhere else. Well, if none will help us we must help ourselves, and commend us to God."

THREE

Run for Life

BUT all was too late.

That very night, Ursulet and Jeanne, in their big half-deserted dortoir, heard the thundering of a great log against the main outer door, and the crash, and the cries of the house-carles in the outer yard.

"It's the Saxons!" Ursulet cried. "Get up—"

Their clothes were simple—the smock over which the gown and bodice went was like the one they slept in, indeed only a delicately brought-up girl would change into a different one for sleeping. This was Jeanne's undoing, for she threw off her night smock and reached for her day one, while Ursulet kept her night smock on but quickly put on her shoes. So that Ursulet was at least in smock and shoes, but Jeanne was naked, when the door splintered and fell in, and a great creature burst into the room. It was all covered with tawny hair, like a bear—Ursulet thought with terror of Jeanne's dream of a bear, but this was a man. He seized Jeanne, smothering her in horrible hair, and fell to the floor with her. Ursulet did not wait to see more. Afterwards, long afterwards, she reproached herself for having fled away and left her friend to her fate, but she could not have saved her. She slipped through the door that the raider had broken down, and rushed down the stairs, out into the courtyard. Everywhere she went was terror, confusion and ghastliness. Numbers of great hairy men were everywhere. They were carrying off the altar candlesticks, the chalices, the lamps. One of the nuns stood desperately in front of the aumbry where the sacred Host was kept; a Saxon thrust her aside and wrenched the aumbry, which was silver-gilt, out of the wall with his sword, while the next behind him seized the nun and began tearing the clothes off her. Two Saxons held the Abbess, her cropped head unveiled—a third swung his sword under her chin. Ursulet, in a moment of awed fascination, saw the head fall and roll away, and the blood gush down over the white habit—Everywhere was pools of blood and splashes of blood on the walls, and bodies whom Ursulet had known as live people lying like bundles of soiled clothes—And from somewhere came the smell of fire and the crackle of mounting flames.

Ursulet ran across the courtyard, not stopping to heed what she saw, and made for the gateway—the great door was lying in fragments, shattered by a log used as a battering ram; four house-carles lay dead around it, but it had no living guardian—the Saxons were all further inside the convent, looting, killing and raping. With terror behind her, Ursulet ran through the gateway, and on and on, along the road that led from the convent. At first she heard pursuing feet behind her, then they fell away, but still she ran on. For far too long, she could hear the savage shouts, the screams, the crashes, and smell the smoke of the burning. It was dark still, before daybreak, but the skies soon paled towards morning; and when at last she stopped running, the first light was in the sky. She stopped through sheer exhaustion, and threw herself down on the grass by the side of the track.

She had no idea where she was, still less where she was to go; one thing only was certain, she could not go back to the convent. And there she was, in the cold daybreak, in her shift and her shoes, without a roof or a bed, without a penny, without a friend. Nothing, nothing, nothing.

Worse than nothing—the world was full of ogres.

While she lay there the rain began to fall, and this was the last misery. She crouched in the ditch, her fair hair plastered to her head, the raindrops mingling with the tears on her cheeks, her only garment sodden and clotted with mud.

Then she heard the whistle. It was far off but clear and somehow significant—somehow alluring. Like a bird's note but much sweeter. It sounded again and again. It changed, bit by bit, into a kind of barbaric, up-and-down warbling tune, that seemed to call her to follow it; and as all directions were the same to her now, she got up and followed where it led. It seemed to come from the depths of the forest that bordered the road; the trees were heavy with late summer leaves and dripping with the rain, but they smelled sweet. Deeper and deeper into the wood the piping led her; one could hardly say there was a path, but there were openings between the trees where it was possible to penetrate. And at last the music led her to a clearing, and in the clearing was a neat little hut, that might have been a hermit's. But it was much prettier than any hermit would own; it was decorated with shells laid out in patterns, and creeping flowers climbed all over it; there was a bright flower-garden in front of it, and each of its four little glazed windows had its window-box of flowers. It was a reassuring and heartening sight, and Ursulet hastened towards it, sure that nothing but good could live in such a pretty house.

The door opened, and there came out a handsome woman, it might be about forty years old, very tall and full of life; her hair was jet-black, and her complexion pale and yet rich, like thick cream. She wore a flowing dress of white silk, with a very beautiful gold girdle and gold border, and many other ornaments of gold, and golden sandals. And she opened the door to poor forlorn Ursulet as if she had expected her.

"Oh, come in, come in!" she exclaimed. "My poor child, what a state you're in. But I was looking out for you. I know who you are, you see."

This seemed strange to Ursulet, but the lady put an arm round her and drew her into the house. And once inside the house, everything was different—this was no cottage, but a rich palace, a vast palace—how was it that Ursulet had thought of it as a cottage? It was such a place as she had heard of in romances but never seen. The walls were panelled with marble, polished and gleaming; carpets covered the shining floors; soft light shone from concealed lamps, and braziers warmed the air with the scent of perfumed gums. Quiet smiling maidservants removed Ursulet's wet shift, and clothed her in a beautiful dress of sky-blue and gold, and replaced her soaking sandals with soft warm slippers. Then they led her to a table, where the lady in white served her with delicious food and drink. The maidservants said no word, but vanished. After a while Ursulet began to find words.

"Who are you, kind lady?"

"That you will find out in time," her benefactress said. "Let it suffice that *I* know who *you* are. I am very interested in you, and I am watching over you to help you recover your kingdom."

"My kingdom?" Ursulet looked up sharply.

"Yes, of course, for you are King Arthur's daughter. But we must be careful. You are set in the midst of many and great dangers—you know that, don't you?"

"I do indeed," she said, remembering what the Abbess had said to her—and then when she recalled how she had last seen the Abbess, she shuddered and felt sick.

"But never fear," said the strange lady, and put a glass of sweet cordial to her lips. "I am your friend. Come now, do you like my palace? Come and walk through it—there are gardens beyond, and fountains with floating lilies, and groves of oranges." And she led her on through fresh delights.

"I think it's wonderful, wonderful!" cried Ursulet. "And you're so kind—"

"All this can be yours," said the strange lady. "All this, and your own rightful kingdom too. Only you should swear fealty to me. Will you?" And she looked into Ursulet's eyes with what seemed like pure friendship. "Simply put your hands between mine," and she stretched out her hands, "and say: I swear to be your liege vassal, to do your bidding, to live or die, here or hereafter, till the world shall end." She stood expectant, but Ursulet drew back.

"I don't think so—yet," she said. "Not till I know who you are, and what you want me to do."

"You must trust me," said the lady. "Cannot you do that?"

"No—I'm sorry," said Ursulet, in some confusion. "I don't want to be rude to you, in any way—you've been so kind, but so big a promise, without knowing anything. . . ."

The lady frowned. "You disappoint me. Well, in that case I shall have to send you back whence you came—and that wasn't very pleasant, remember?—Still, my offer remains open, if you should think better of your decision. Wear my token, and you will certainly see me again," and she placed around Ursulet's neck a silver chain on which was a little charm in the shape of a pentagram, with the middle point downwards. And then, suddenly, everything was gone—the lady, her palace, Ursulet's new clothes and all. She was back by the roadside, in the rain, with her streaming hair and her wet shift. Whether she had indeed eaten and drunk, and been rested and warmed, she could not tell—she was certainly very cold and hungry. But round her neck was the chain with the reversed pentagram. And it was only then that she remembered that it took the place of a little gold cross that her father had hung about her neck long years ago, and which had never left her till she had dropped it, she supposed, in her flight.

FOUR

The Jutes

And now she was more desolate than ever. There seemed to be nowhere to go but along the road, so she plodded forward. And then suddenly a man sprang at her from the roadside. Like an animal, she ran without looking round to see him clearly, and just evaded his grasp; but she got the impression of a thickset, heavy man in a sheepskin cap, with a sheepskin over his back that was about all the clothing he had, and a wide, red, stupid face. Not a Saxon, but what of that? Every bit as bad, and pelting after her, uttering cries of imbecile desire. She ran and ran, and eventually distanced him, but she could still hear him pursuing. And now in front of her was the first sign of human habitation she had seen since she ran from the convent—not, of course, counting vision and glamoury. This seemed to be a rough homestead, a group of four or five untidy thatched huts enclosed within a thorn fence. She made for this—there might be refuge here. There was a gap left in the fence, and she ran through and approached the huts. They were connected by rough paths of large stones, making a causeway through what was otherwise a sea of mud.

As Ursulet approached one of the huts, a woman came out right in front of her—a big ugly woman, immensely fat and rotund. She was carrying a brimming bowl in both hands, probably full of curds, and as she was within arm's reach of Ursulet she stumbled and fell forward. With an instinctive movement like catching a thrown ball, Ursulet caught the bowl from her and held it safely, as the woman measured her length on the muddy ground. Ursulet stepped quickly inside the hut—it was cluttered and filthy—and with some difficulty found a place to put the bowl down; then she went back to the woman, who was still lying on the ground and moaning. Ursulet examined her carefully, but could not see any injury—and then it suddenly dawned on her with a shock that the woman was about to give birth to a baby.

Living as she had in the convent, Ursulet had never even seen a pregnant woman before; but once, very daring and in great secrecy, with the connivance of a kitchen-maid, she and Jeanne had watched a cat have kittens. She knew very little indeed about birth, and worst of all, she did not understand a word of the woman's language. She appeared to be a Jute—there were settlements of Jutes towards the seacoast, and they were said to be not quite as bad as the Angles, nor anything like as terrible as the Saxons, in fact almost human but that they didn't speak the Celtic tongue. The woman, rolling over on the ground, jabbered away in her own language, and with gestures and looks implored Ursulet not to leave her. It seemed to Ursulet that certain things needed doing, such as to get the woman into a hut and if possible to bed: so she helped her to her feet—the woman was remarkably heavy and inert—and supported her into the nearest hut, and got her into the kind of shallow box full of straw that was evidently the proper lying-in bed.

The Jutish woman made a great many things clear enough by signs—she herself knew all about childbirth anyhow, having had six children (so she indicated on her fingers), of whom four had died. Her need, it appeared, was not so much for expert help as just for someone to fetch things for her, to put water on to boil, to get in more straw, to unpack the swaddling clothes from a wooden chest—and also to give her moral support and hold her hand in the crisis of the pains. She gave Ursulet to understand that it would be quite a time before the baby was born, and indicated in the meantime that she might help herself to milk, bread, cheese and bacon and dry her garment at the fire, which she gratefully did. Ursulet sat comfortably enough on a stool between the straw bed and the fire, her back against the wall, and rested at last. Then suddenly the door cracked open and the woman's husband came in, and Ursulet sprang to her feet—it was her pursuer. He gave a long chuckling "O-ho-o-o!" and shot out his arm for her; but his wife jerked herself upright in the straw, and threw a volley of harsh guttural words at him—rising step by step to a shriek—then for good measure she reached out and seized a large log of firewood, and before sinking back in another pain, flung it at him. He went out of the hut quicker than he had come in. The patient fell back in the straw, and between moans made a long and impassioned speech, clearly about the said husband. It hardly needed translating.

When the birth took place, the woman herself seemed to know exactly what to do, and showed Ursulet what needed to be done. Presently the husband reappeared, and with him the midwife, a gnarled and witchlike old woman. But the baby was already born and yelling heartily. It was a boy, and quite successfully brought into the world, as the midwife was the first to admit. To Ursulet's delight, the midwife spoke the Celtic tongue as well as the Saxon.

"You a midwife?" she said to Ursulet. "You're too young."

"Oh no—I just happened to be here. I ran away—the Saxons burnt the convent."

"The Saxons? Ha, yes. You'd do better to stay here and work for Hertha and Burl. They're all right. Yes, Burl is a randy beast, but Hertha won't let him touch you, she's as jealous as the devil. You'll get food and a roof over your head, and be safe from the Saxons." Her eyes strayed to the charm about Ursulet's neck. "Here, what's this? Are you one of them?"

"I don't know what you mean."

"Oh, of course you wouldn't say so, but you needn't be afraid to tell me—I'm on good terms with plenty of them though I'm not one myself—lots of people would say I am, for they'll say that of anyone who knows anything. You're young, but I'd say you were an apprentice."

"I'm not a witch, if that's what you mean," said Ursulet.

"Then why do you wear the Witches' Star?"

"Is it? I didn't know—somebody gave it me—"

"Did they so? Then I'd counsel you to hide it if you don't want to be taken for a witch. Oh, one more bit of advice. Keep close inside this hut tonight, and as near as possible to Hertha. Old Burl will have all his friends in to drink to the child, and if you don't know what that will mean, you soon will. But no matter how drunk he is, he's afraid of Hertha. She makes him hold his wassail in the other hut, so they won't touch you if you stay where Hertha can see you."

So at last Ursulet lay down to rest on a heap of straw in the corner of the hut, amidst indescribable muddle and squalor; and she hoped to sleep at last, but was too jangled and strung up by all that she had been through. For hours she listened to the Jutes yelling over their drink in the other hut, the baby crying at intervals, and Hertha snoring. So began the first of many, many nights, and many days, as unpaid drudge among the Jutes, without a name or any to recall her identity.

FIVE

The Knighting of Ambris

HEN Ambris's father, Gawain le Jeune, was slain in Arthur's last great battle, the light of the sun went out for Ambris, and for his mother, and for many besides. There were so many that died there— not only Young Gawain, but Ambris's grandfather the gentle Gareth, and his three great-uncles, Gawain the Elder, Gaheris and Agravaine. Some said that Gawain and Gaheris had been killed earlier, almost accidentally, in the melee that went on when Guinevere was rescued by Lance- lot from execution by burning; but no one quite knew the rights of it. Least of all Ambris, who was not much more than seven years old. But he knew that they were gone, with Arthur the King and all the Round Table, and he was all the comfort left to the red-haired Lady Vivian. His grandmother Leonie of Lyonesse was so broken by the grief of losing both her husband and her son that she died soon after. But none witnessed the grief of the Lady Lynett.

The Lady Lynett was not like anyone else at all. Since fifty years old she had not changed much. She rode about the country on one of King Arthur's own black horses (which men said were cross-bred from the tall Eastern horses which the Romans brought over), sometimes with an attendant dwarf, sometimes all alone, as a kind of special messenger between King Arthur and his knights. She had been doing this ever since she was young. She it was who, when her sister Leonie, the Lady Lyonesse, had been be- sieged by the Knight of the Red Launddes, had ridden to Camelot to ask the King for a champion for her sister, and had brought back Gareth. All the world knows how un- mercifully she had treated him on that journey—for she was deeply in love with him. Of course he married Leonie, as Lynett had foreseen he would; and King Arthur had ever so kindly bestowed Lynett's hand on Gareth's brother

Gaheris. What wonder that the marriage was not successful? It was as well she had not been given to Gawain, for he was subject to sudden rages, and might quite well have lopped off her head in one of them. Gaheris had left her on their wedding night and carefully avoided meeting her again; and Lynett could have gone back to live with her sister—and Gareth, and their son Gawain the Younger; but this she would not do. So it was at this time she became Arthur's "Damosel Errante," riding about the country for months together, carrying letters, taking confidential messages to outlying rulers, turning up at the most unexpected moments. There was a bag on her saddle-bow, which might contain letters, or golden coins, or now and then the decapitated head of a man, with a demand for vengeance, or a story of vengeance accomplished. In appearance she was an impressive woman even in her sixties, having a well-shaped face and a clear skin, though very sunburnt, and bright brown eyes. She was taller than many men, and sat her horse with a back as straight as a soldier's; she rode about wearing a soldier's old leather hauberk plated with metal, and a wide skirt of coarse grey frieze, and great boots up to her knees. She wore her grey hair streaming down her back, with a red kerchief tied over it and caught back behind her ears—so that people should see she was a woman, she said, and accord her the privileges of her sex. In King Arthur's time she rode fearlessly up and down the country; now the land was not so safe, but still she rode up and down, and took her chance on what she met. Robbers and outlaws, all knew her as a remarkable healer of wounds and sickness—this in itself would sometimes have been enough to brand a woman as a witch, but the outlaws valued her, and perhaps feared her acid tongue. What errands she rode on now that the King was dead was her own business.

Ambris heard her come in, after one of her long absences—she strode through the open hall, and into the panelled soler where he was sitting disconsolate and idle by the fire. She slapped her big leather gloves down on the table.

"Come," she said. "We're going on a journey, you and I. Tomorrow morning."

Nobody gainsaid Aunt Lynett, least of all her grand-nephew, though he was now eighteen. The next morning, after a leave-taking with his mother that Lynett mercilessly cut short, they were out on the roads together—he on his good bay hackney, she on the great black horse of Arthur's stable. It was said she had outlived three of them.

They rode all day with but short pauses for rest, and in the evening (it was late sad January) came to a place which seemed to be more than half under water, for all along the side of the road, sometimes on both sides, stretched pale still meres, bordered with thick beds of reeds. No hills or trees anywhere, only the flat sheets of water, and the reeds, and the road winding on a narrow causeway. In some places there were bays among the reeds, where wild-fowl of all kinds gave life to the scene—ducks playing in the waters, moorhens, swans, and once a white spectral pelican. But in other places, and increasingly as they went on, the water was deserted, quiet, broken only by a rising fish or a frog. The sun had disappeared into clouds, and set without glow or colour, and the meres gleamed as coldly as mirrors in an empty room.

Then, while there was still faint light in the sky, Lynett reined in her horse and they halted. She pointed, where far away a solitary hill rose, at a towering pointed hill with a strange turret on its top.

"There," she said. "There is Avalon, the holy Ynys Witrin."

"Do we go there?" he asked, almost in a whisper, for the name and the sight had struck awe into him.

"No. We stay here. Dismount now."

And as he dismounted he saw, almost as if it had previously been invisible, a group of low dark buildings beside him. One was a chapel—it had the pointed shape, the belfry above, and a subdued, flickering light coming from the candles that burnt on the altar within. Another was a rough reed-thatched hut, and from it came firelight; and a man stepped out and greeted Lynett with courtly formality. The words and gestures suited oddly with the wild, cold, barbaric scene by the bleak waters at the fall of night.

The man did not seem like an ordinary hermit—he wore no monastic cowl or habit, but the rough leather garments that a knight would wear under his armour. His head was not shaven, but bald with age, except for the white locks that hung behind his ears and on his neck; his brows were bushy, and a thin, straggling, forked beard fell down over his breast. His face was mild and calm, and his eyes such as Ambris felt he would trust entirely. The old man was girt with a leather belt, studded with bronze, that held a long sword in a threadbare scabbard; and behind him, in his hut, the full armour of a Knight of the Round Table hung in order on the wall.

They stepped inside the hut, a small enough place but neat, and lighted by the fire; and Lynett put her hand on Ambris's shoulder.

"This is the boy," she said. "Ambris, my young kinsman, this is Sir Bedivere, the last of the true Knights of the Round Table."

With tears in his eyes, Ambris knelt and kissed the old man's hand.

Sir Bedivere smiled, and drew him to his feet.

"He'll do," he said. "Tall and has a look of the Orkneymen. Is he old enough?"

"He's eighteen."

"It will suffice. *She* must be nearly two years older, of course, and we must not wait too long. I think it is time."

"That is why I have brought him to you."

"Yes, I think it is time, or nearly so. See here," and from the back of the hut he brought what looked like a long garland of leaves, some parched dry, some only wilting as if newly plucked. There were bunches of different kinds of leaves, tied at regular intervals along a piece of cord. Lynett sat down on a stool and examined each bunch in detail.

"Let me see—birch, ash, willow—that's Belinus. Hawthorn, holly, hazel—Hauteric. Vine ivy, willow—Margansius. Elder, reed, rowan—Ringel. And each one with an acorn on a twig, to show they stand pledged to Arthur's heir." She went on counting over the leaves. Every combination of leaves and twigs spelled out a name to her, and there were maybe thirty bunches of leaves in the garland. Over some she chuckled with pleasure—others, she looked sharply up at Bedivere and questioned him, but always she was satisfied.

"Have they all been here?" she said.

"They have all been here, and made their vow, to support the lawful house of Arthur, if his true heir can be found."

"Not Mordred and his brood?"

"I said his lawful heir. We know who that is—the true born daughter by Guinevere his queen. The Princess Ursulet—if she can be found."

At the mention of the Princess, Ambris lifted his head and gave a smothered exclamation. The other two turned, looked at him, looked back at each other with raised eyebrows, but said nothing. The firelight flickered on the bare walls of the hut. Sir Bedivere rose and made a simple meal for them—rye bread, cheese, cresses and small ale, served in wooden vessels and platters. Hungry though Ambris was, he was too oppressed by the solemnity and gravity of his companions to eat much; but he drank the thin tasteless ale gratefully, for his mouth was dry.

When they had fed and rested, Sir Bedivere broke the silence.

"Ambris, my son—are you prepared for the honour of knighthood?"

"What, me?—I mean—here and now, sir?"

"Here and now. We need you to go on the quest for Arthur's lost daughter, and for that, you must be knighted. I alone am left of the true Company of the Round Table, and so I alone have the right to confer knighthood on you. I wish indeed it could be done as in the old days—with all the knights here, and the ladies, and the monks chanting, the tapers and the banners, and Arthur himself to lay the sword on your shoulder—but since that cannot be, I must do the best I can for you."

"I am not shriven," the boy said, his eyes on the ground. "Will you shrive me?"

"No, I cannot do that, for I am not a priest. Tomorrow the priest will come over from Avalon, as he does every morning, and you shall be shriven and houselled. But for now, you will be purified in another way. Go out now, and down to the side of the mere, and bathe yourself in the water."

"What, now? In the dark—"

"It is not so very dark. There is a moon behind the clouds."

"Must I—must I go alone?"

"Of course—who should go with you? Look, you must stand in the water by the bank—it is not very deep—naked, mind you—and plunge right in, over your head and all. Every hair of you. You understand?"

The boy nodded mutely.

"Here is a linen cloth to dry your body, and you will not put your clothes on again, but clothe yourself in this tunic of white wool. It's warm enough. And then come back here to me."

Ambris said, "Yes, sir," very quietly and shakily, and went out into the dark. In spite of the moon behind the clouds, it seemed very dark to him, very cold and frightening. At the edge of the gleaming mere, trembling, he took off his clothes, and as he did so, the glittering eyes of a toad came into his sight, on a corner of the bank—a very large toad, and it seemed to be watching him. He didn't like that toad one bit.

He laid his clothes on the wet grass of the bank, carefully placing the towel and the white wool tunic on the top of the pile. Then, shrinking and bare, he stepped into the muddy water. It was intensely cold, and slippery underfoot, with sharp stones and submerged snags lacerating his feet. Gritting his teeth, he plunged under the water and then scrambled quickly out. The woollen tunic felt gratefully warm as he put it on, and slipped his shoes on his scratched feet. In a few minutes he was at the door of the hut, where Bedivere waited him.

"Not your shoes," said Bedivere. "Take those off again."

Now he led him, cold as he was and with his hair still dripping, to the little chapel adjoining the cell. It was a bare little room of stone, with an opening to the westward that had no door to close it, and a small unglazed window high up to the eastward, under which was a rough stone altar, covered with a cloth, with a bronze cross and candlesticks. The two candles burned steadily. In front of the altar was a faldstool. On the altar lay a sword, and below was piled a knight's full suit of armour.

"Here," said Bedivere, "you are to keep your vigil of knighthood. Kneel here at the faldstool, and fix your eyes on the altar. You will stay there until you hear me ring the bell at daybreak, and you must *not* look around. You must not turn your head even once. Not even once, you understand, no matter what you may see or hear.—Now let us pray for your dedication."

So Bedivere left him, in the dark little cell, kneeling, resting his arms on the faldstool, staring at the dull gleam of the bronze cross lit by the candles. He heard Bedivere's footsteps die away beyond the open doorway.

As he settled to his vigil he recalled what his father had told him about the time when he kept his own vigil of knighthood at Camelot—how first of all Mordred and his ribald friends had tried to frighten him by making shadow-pictures on the wall in front of him, and had run away laughing, but he had to keep from looking round; and then how dreadful thoughts assailed him, and took the visible forms of demons, a hideous old man, a beautiful woman with the body of a serpent.

But he, Ambris, must not ask for trouble by thinking about such things. He would say his Pater and Ave, and another Pater and Ave, and not fall asleep. . . .

A soft footfall behind him startled him into full atten-tion. Very soft and light—not old Bedivere's and certainly not his great-aunt's. Someone came in through the doorway behind him—without moving his head he tried to turn his eyes as far as he could first to right and then to left. By the corner of his left eye he could almost see the intruder—something white-robed, soft, glimmering, female. She passed behind him again, and he could glimpse her from the corner of his right eye. A very faint breath of perfume came to him.

He brought his eye back to the centre of the bronze cross, and spoke to the presence.

"Whoever you are, come out here in front, and let me see you."

There was a rustle of soft draperies, and she came round him and stood between him and the altar. She was strangely beautiful, tall, pale, robed in white, with intensely black hair.

"Since you ask me to stand in the holy place I am able to do so," she said, smiling. "That is courteous of you. But I don't think you need go on kneeling there very much longer. You are tired. I am sent to bid you take a rest."

He drew a long breath and prepared to rise from the faldstool—then he checked.

"Thank you," he said, "but I am not to rise till I hear the bell. I do not think it is time yet."

"Oh, have it your own way," she laughed. "If you want to cling to these old-fashioned forms. . . . You want to find the Princess, and restore her to Arthur's throne, do you not? Well, let me tell you, your dear old godsibs in there, Sir Bedivere and the Lady your great-aunt Lynett—they don't know where she is. But I know! Oh yes, I know!"

"Do you indeed?" He leant forward, gripping the rail of the faldstool. "Then tell me where to find her."

34

"Fair and softly!" The red lips laughed at him. "Yes I know where she is. And I will tell you, nay, I will lead you to her and help you to set her on Arthur's throne—for a price."

"What is your price?" he whispered.

"Come with me and I will show you," and she sidled round again to his left, and up till she stood by his left shoulder. "Come with me. It will do you more good than all this ancient formality. Get up off your knees, and turn round, and come with me, and I will tell you what my price is."

"No," he said, keeping his eyes firmly on the altar. "I don't believe you, and I'm not going to be persuaded to leave here. Please leave me alone."

"Indeed? But you must believe that I know where the Princess is. You will not find her without me."

"I don't trust you, and I don't believe you."

"Young sir," she said, coming round to his right again (so she had made two circles widdershins around him), "you are not as courteous as a knight ought to be."

"I'm sorry," he said. "But I have my orders." But his voice was beginning to weaken. She crossed in front of him, and as she passed he could see her golden ornaments, and how her feet moved in golden sandals. Then she went to his left and stood again behind him.

"Ambris, Ambris," she said, very low, so that he only just heard her. "Look at me, Ambris." She came closer, and breathed on his neck, so that his hair bristled upright. "Ambris—look at me. I am very beautiful, Ambris. You may not get the chance to see me again. Turn and look at me—Ambris, Ambris. . . ."

And now indeed it was hard for him to resist—just to look round once, just once—

And then the cock crew—and reminded him of many things.

He clung to the faldstool, crying wildly, "Oh, no betrayal! no betrayal!"—and then the footsteps suddenly ceased, and the sense of presence and the warmth and perfume were gone. Yet he did not venture to turn around. Instead, he lay against his folded arms on the faldstool, as if swooning. Then in the little belfry above him he heard the bell ring, and Sir Bedivere came in and laid his hand on his shoulder. He looked behind now, and saw that the daylight was coming in through the door of the chapel.

Bedivere said no word to him, but turned the faldstool round so that Ambris could sit and rest himself against it. Then came Lynett, and laid a rich embroidered cloth on the altar, and set up six silver candlesticks and a silver cross in place of the bronze one, and brought holy water and a smoking censer. First she took the holy water, and Bedivere the censer, and they made purification, and censed and sprinkled the armour and the sword; then Bedivere put the armour on Ambris—the breastplate, the belt, the spurs, the helmet, the shield, and lastly the sword. And he made Ambris kneel, and repeat the vows of knighthood; and finally Bedivere drew his own great sword, and held it point upward, so that the rays of the morning sun ran along its blade—then lowered it till the blade rested on Ambris's shoulder.

"In the Name of God, and of King Arthur who does not die," he said, "I make you, now and forever, a knight of the Round Table." Then he raised him by the right hand, saying, "Rise, Sir Ambrosius."

And so Ambris became a knight.

And as he walked from the chapel with unsteady steps, Lynett stood before him.

"Since there is no man to do this for you," she said, "I must. Greetings, Sir Ambrosius, and be thou a good knight" —and her great leathery hand lashed out and caught him a stinging blow on the cheek.

He stood bewildered, his hand to his cheek.

"I'm sorry," he said. "What was that for?"

Now she caught both hands in her own, and kissed him, and he saw that there were tears in her eyes.

"That is the knightly buffet, my son. It is a dear privilege, and carries all my blessing with it."

And he remembered how he had heard that the old Gawain, his great-uncle, had done the like to his father, the young Gawain, at his knighting, and knocked him down, so that he swooned; and he smiled, and pressed Lynett's arm that was linked in his.

"Rather you than my great-uncle, dear aunt," he said, and they both laughed for the first time in those two days.

❦

SIX

The New Knight

THE priest arrived from Avalon, and Mass was said in the little chapel, as was right and proper; and then Ambris was allowed to sleep. When he woke, Bedivere and Lynett had prepared as festive a breakfast for him as a hermit might—frumenty and cream, and eggs, and honeycomb—and afterwards just a small glass of sweet red wine for each of them, to drink to the new-made knight. And after the solemnity and strain of the ceremony, in the light cheerful morning with the birds singing, they relaxed and were cheerful, and Ambris discovered that these two, immensely old as they seemed to him, could be merry company. And after a while, he ventured to tell them of what he had seen and heard during his vigil—and at once they were grave again.

"I thought she was dead," Lynett said.

"No, beings such as she are not slain so easily," said Bedivere. "They say that Merlin bade the young Gawain spare her life, but banish her from the land of living men."

"But who *is* she?" Ambris asked.

"She is Morgan le Fay, the mistress of all illusion and glamoury, skilled above all others in making that seem which is not. She was mighty for evil in King Arthur's day. She is also some sort of kin to you," said Lynett, "for she is the sister of Vivian-Nimuë, who was your mother's grandmother, Merlin himself being your mother's grandfather. Morgan is also the sister of Morgause, the Queen of Orkney, who was the mother of Gawain, Gaheris, Agravaine, and Gareth your grandfather."

"And of Mordred also," said Bedivere.

"And of Mordred also. . . . She will try every possible means to destroy the daughter of Arthur. It seems she seeks to destroy you also. She wishes to rule Britain herself, or through her creatures—such as Mordred. If she can, she will place Mordred, or one of his sons, on the throne. But we, Ambris—Sir Bedivere and I, we know the knights, barons, and earls too, that are ready to rise in support of Arthur's daughter, if she can be found. And that is for you to do."

"I will, of course, if I can," he said, "but why me?"

"Bedivere must remain here, as a centre upon which the well-wishers may rally—he is the hub of the wheel. And I," said Lynett, "it is too well known that I was Arthur's messenger. If I sought her out now, I would be followed, and would lead the enemy to her. You, I think, will not be suspected yet, unless the spirit of the witch-woman has means to lead Mordred to you. You may escape Mordred's vigilance. But there is no one else. *You* must find her, and bring her here, whence we will go to Avalon, where our friends will muster their armies. The true men, whose names I know, are recorded in my garland of the tree-Ogham. Will you do this?"

"Certainly I will, God helping me. But where do I start looking for her?"

"You could go first to Amesbury, where lives Melior, a priest, the last man that knew Merlin. He was present when Guinevere died, and from him you may learn something."

Bedivere turned abruptly. A man stood in the door of the hut.

"What is it, Wulf?"

"He's coming, sir—a great lord on a horse, with two serving men behind—it could be the Earl Mordred. Three miles off as the road winds—I cut across the bog before them—"

Lynett was already stripping down the garland from where it hung, and cramming it under her wide skirt.

"Hide the boy," she said. "Ambris, you musn't be seen. Get in here," and she uncovered a hole under a heap of firewood at the farthest recess of the hut—"Don't, whatever you see or hear—*whatever* happens—don't come out. Bedivere will meet him. I'll take the horses and hide in the reeds—I know how to, well enough. They won't find *this*," and she touched the garland that rustled under her skirt.

Bedivere had taken Ambris's armour off him, all but the belt and sword; Ambris was now dressed in his leather jerkin and hose, which would not rattle. He drew himself into the hole under the firewood, and Bedivere piled the faggots in front of him. He could hear, but could see nothing. Tensely listening, he heard horses outside the hut, and the heavy footsteps of three men.

A heavy voice, between unctuous and brutal, greeted Bedivere.

"Well, if it isn't our old friend Bedivere! A long time since we met, old knight. You'd hardly believe the difficulty I've had in finding you.—Oh, sit down, sit down. A snug little hermitage you have here—and a lot of interesting things in it." The heavy steps went round the hut as if searching. "Not many books—no parchments now? Or letters? No scrolls of names, for instance? No?"

Ambris heard a metallic clank, as if the newcomer was handling the old knight's armour.

"Ah, you keep your old Round Table equipment. I see. Very touching sentiment. But what's this? A *new* suit of armour? Well now, who might this be for?"

"My lord Mordred," came Bedivere's voice, "since you ask me, it's for the nephew of my priest that comes over from Avalon—his fancies dwell much on the old days—"

"Do you know, I'm not much inclined to believe in your priest or his nephew?—Men, seize him." There was the sound of a scuffle. Then the voice went on. "Now, don't you think you'd better admit what I know already—that you're conspiring, together with that old witch Lynett, to set a pretender on Arthur's throne? Oh, you needn't shut your mouth and roll your eyes. I know it all, you see, and can wait here till I catch all your fellow-conspirators. Only I'd rather know their names, and also who this armour is for—and I think you'll tell me very shortly."

There was a tense silence in the hut. Ambris wished he could only see what was happening.

"Will you tell now?"

No answer, but a hiss of breath drawn in sharply, and then a long shuddering sigh, and a horrible smell of burning flesh.

Ambris could bear it no longer. He broke from his hiding-place, sword in hand, scattering the firewood—the men-at-arms, taken by surprise, put their hands up to ward off the shower of twigs. All on the spring of the one impulse, without stopping, Ambris thrust his sword into the back of the man who was stooping over Bedivere, scooped up the half-unconscious Bedivere in his left arm as if he had been a child, was out of the hut, on to the back of one of the three horses tethered there, and away, thundering down the causeway.

A man rose out of the reeds and ran beside him—he recognised Wulf, Bedivere's man. "Come this way, sir," he said. "Follow me, I know the secret tracks." Ambris listened for pursuit behind him, but for the moment there was none. He followed Wulf into the narrow tracks among the reeds, supporting Bedivere on his saddle-bow against his breast. What a mercy the old man was so thin and light, he thought.

Presently they reached a little island closed round with willows, into which the narrow causeway led. In the middle of the willows was Lynett with her horse and his.

She cried out when she saw Ambris and Bedivere.

"What has happened? Why are you both here?"

"The young fool broke out of covert," Bedivere growled, slipping to the ground and unsteadily finding his feet.

"Sir Bedivere was being tortured," exclaimed Ambris. "I couldn't sit by and hear it—*I couldn't.*"

"But my son," cried Lynett, "all depended upon Mordred not seeing you. We are undone! He knows you now— are you not pursued?"

"Oh—I seem to have done the wrong thing. I'm sorry," said Ambris, red-faced and looking at the ground. "I just couldn't let them torture him."

"I was enduring Mordred's rough questioning as best I might," grumbled Bedivere, "when our young jack-hare here breaks covert and runs for it, taking me with him. And now his face is known and all's marred."

"But sir," said Ambris, "I don't think he ever saw my face—I doubt if his men did either. You see, before I caught you up, I thrust my sword in his back, and as he fell forward his men ran to catch him—and perhaps that is why they have not pursued us yet."

Lynett's face cleared. "You did? You thrust your sword through Mordred's back? God send you killed him!"

"I fear not. It wasn't a very knightly blow, for my first. I don't think I put it through his heart—only through his thick buttock!"

Bedivere and Lynett shouted with laughter together.

"Oh, well done, lad! Pity it wasn't higher, but no matter! He won't sit his horse for many months—and how he'll curse—" Lynett slapped her knee and rocked to and fro.

"No, with any luck they'll not have noticed your face, and we've got a start of them. But we won't stay here. Come, whether or no, you must make for Amesbury, but go roundabout. Bedivere and I will go to Avalon, but you mustn't show yourself there yet."

Ambris turned to Bedivere, who was leaning heavily on his arm.

"Let me help you to my own horse, sir," he said. "Did the villain hurt you much? What did he do to you?"

"We won't speak of it. But—thank you, son, thank you. You came in time, when all's said and done. And your aunt has the names safe and sound—under that petticoat of hers. Come, let's be going."

SEVEN

The Slave of the Jutes

"WIFE," said Burl the Jute, as they snorted and shuffled together in their straw bed, "I'm going to sell that girl Urz'l. Grimfrith the Saxon will give a cow for her."

"You're not! She's a good girl, and useful."

"She's no use. Willibrod is weaned long ago, and you'll have no more children. What, do you think you should have a body-woman to run after you and comb your hair, as if you were a lady?"

"Indeed! and who's to carry water, and feed the swine, and herd the geese, and tend the hens, and wash your filthy shirts when you'll part up with them, and mend Willibrod's clothes when he tears them, and sweep out the byre, and—"

"Oh, peace! Look you, scolding shrew that you are, the cow we shall get for her will have a calf, which is more than this Urz'l will ever do—"

"Not for want of your trying, you wicked old man."

"Never mind that—but what's the good of a girl who won't take a man at all? Twenty years old and still a maid! It's not in nature—it's all wrong. She's losing her looks, too—she's too thin. Well, if Grimfrith fancies her, let him try, that's all. And this cow, I tell you, she will have a calf, and we can trade that for another girl, younger and of even more use to you."

"More use to you, you mean, you filthy old lecher. That's what it is—you're tired of this one saying no to you, and she's past her best, and you'll have one young and willing. I know you, you old Nithing."

"You be silent, or I'll take my strap to you. I say she shall go to Grimfrith, and go she shall. Mind you, these Saxons don't keep their slaves long."

"So I've heard. I'm sorry for the maid, then."

"Saxons have no patience—a word and a blow, and often the blow's a heavy one. They can't be bothered with them. That's why they don't often take prisoners in battle—they don't find them worth the trouble of keeping. Especially the clever ones—they die the first."

"Then I say it's a pity to let the maid go to such as they. She's been a good girl to me these six years."

"Oh yes, you're getting soft now, are you? I tell you, I mean to have that cow—it's in calf already, did you know? I mean to have it, and get rid of that Urz'l, so shut up, you."

In the morning, a wet and discouraging spring morning, Ursulet stood by the doorposts looking out on the muddy yard of the farmstead, dimly wondering if there was anything in the world but mud. She was twenty, and very tall and thin—too thin, for her master fed her but poorly and worked her far too hard, and her mistress was much the same, in spite of occasional feeble attempts at kindness that mostly came to nothing. Ursulet wore a cast-off dress of Hertha's, of loosely woven brown linen stuff—a texture not unlike sacking. It was far too big for her, of course, and hung shapelessly on her angular bones; she had tied it up with the straw cord they used to bind the hay-bales. If there were time, she often told herself, she would plait a straw belt—but whenever there was a little bit of time to spare, she was too tired. Her long pale hair was without colour or lustre, and was screwed to the back of her head in a tight bun. Her face was a brickdust brown, in the midst of which her luminous light-grey eyes looked out startlingly. Her feet were as tough as leather, and as brown.

Now she was watching Burl and his neighbour Grimfrith the Saxon walking slowly towards the house.

"Well, there she is," said Burl. "We'll walk over to your place together, and then I'll take the cow back."

"Right," said the Saxon, and seized hold of Ursulet's arm. "Come along now—you belong to me."

Ursulet jibbed, pulling against the unpleasant hand that held her.

"What's this?" she said. "You can't do this to me."

"What, we can't do this to you?" guffawed Burl, and the other man joined in.

"You can't sell me. I'm a free woman. I'm not your slave."

"Not your slave, she says?" roared Burl. "Not your slave—these six years, eh? Not your slave! Why you no-good bundle of bones, who in the devil's name do you think you are, then?"

And who was she? *Who* was she? Ursulet could hardly think, could hardly remember, after six years of no other life but this—only that she was no slave. Then, like a lesson learnt long ago, it came back to her. She drew herself up.

"I am the Princess Ursulet, lawful and only daughter of King Arthur of Britain and his queen Guinevere."

For a moment the two men, and Hertha in the background, stood round-eyed and round-mouthed at her sudden stateliness, then they all roared with laughter.

"Princess, she says! Daughter of King Arthur, she says! Oh, beg your pardon, your royal ladyship!" And Burl swept her a mock bow, and followed it with an obscene gesture. "Wife, we thought she was mad, but we never thought she was as mad as this."

"See what a bargain I'm getting!" shouted Grimfrith. "A royal princess for the price of one cow! Thank you, good neighbour, I'm sure. And now I can call myself King of Britain—that's a good one!"

"Come along, king's daughter," said Burl, and grabbed her at one side while Grimfrith closed up on the other. "See the royal neck-ring we've got for you," and between them, in spite of her struggles, they fastened an iron slave-ring round her neck. There was a chain attached to it, and Grimfrith held the end of the chain. She was as helpless as a puppy on a leash. She fought and struggled with all the strength in her spare wiry body, but the horrible ring bit into her neck and choked her. No use to scream, though she rent the air with her screams. If there were any people within miles, they were only too used to the sound of screams coming from that quarter. She dug her feet into the mud of the path, but her captor dragged her to the ground and she was pulled along by the collar, strangling. In the end, exhausted, she gave up, and trudged along where she was led, her captors still laughing.

She knew exactly what the Saxon would want, as soon as he got her to his house. Which house was the usual one-room hut, even more dirty and untidy than the Jute's, for Grimfrith's wife was dead, and his last woman slave also. There was the box of straw that served for a bed, and he tried to drag her to it as soon as Burl had left with his cow. Having got his cow, Burl was no longer interested in Ursulet. But the moment Grimfrith loosed his hold on Ursulet's chain, having her behind a barred door, Ursulet snatched up a knife from the table, and held it point upwards toward him. He gave back a little at first, but would still have overpowered her, but that he snatched away the upper part of her garment, and there round her neck was the reversed pentagram.

"Oh, good God!" he exclaimed, for he was a Christian of sorts when he remembered it. "The woman's a witch! Burl never told me that." He backed over to the other side of the hut, making first the sign of the Cross, and then that of the Hammer of Thor to make sure.

"Are you a witch, girl?" he asked in rather less than his usual loud tone. She saw her chance and took it.

"Yes, I'm a witch, and if you lay a hand upon me the creeping palsy will take you. The man who lies with me will never be a man again." She pointed two fingers at him, and he shrank back against the wall.

"The Lord between us and all harm! I'll not meddle with a witch. Get out of here. Get out, do you hear?" He groped to the door and unbarred it, then he grabbed a pitchfork, and with the tines each side of her neck thrust her out, slammed the door, and bolted it. She stumbled and slipped in the filthy mud outside the door, but quickly picked herself up, and ran with all her might away from the homestead—anywhere to get away from both the Saxon and the Jute. So far she had escaped; no doubt the two would get together after a while, and Grimfrith would accuse Burl of having sold him a witch, and Hertha would say she had never shown any signs of witchcraft, and then they'd start looking for her again. Grimfrith wouldn't lightly give up the price of a perfectly good cow. But for the moment she was free, so she ran on further into the forest.

EIGHT

Fugitive Again

SHE was a very different fugitive from the one who had fled from the sack of the nunnery, six years past. Then, she had been tenderly reared, soft of flesh, as innocent of the world as one of the Abbess's white rabbits. Now she was hard in every muscle, and the feet that had been so bruised, even in sandals, had never worn sandals since, and were harder bare than many feet in shoes. There was no form of work that was hard, dirty, unpleasant, filthy or tedious to which she was not hardened.

And as to her mind—it might have been expected that the numbing routine of work, exhaustion, sleep—work, exhaustion, sleep—would have atrophied her mind, and made her incapable of either thinking or feeling. But the intellect with which she was born was not so easily killed. When she had recovered from the shock of her violent uprooting, her mind had adapted itself, and made the best of what it had. She had quickly learnt the language of the people around her—that of the Angles, Saxons and Jutes—but she continued to say her prayers in Latin, and sometimes sang the Latin hymns of the convent when Burl was not there to hear her—Hertha and little Willibrod listened to them with wonder. And she talked to herself inside her head in her own Celtic language. Sometimes she spoke it with the midwife, so as not to forget it altogether. There was very little company at the Jutish "Ham," only Burl and Hertha and Willibrod, and sometimes Willibrod's brother and sister, who were grown up and had settlements of their own; sometimes the midwife, and very occasionally a neighbour or two—otherwise, nobody.

There were things that Ursulet could not bear to remember, so much of her convent life was blotted out, together with much that was behind a still earlier barrier—her beautiful mother and her heroic father, and everything before she was six. But some of her convent training remained with her, and set her apart from the grossness of the people around her; and she had a feeling for personal cleanliness which the Jutes ridiculed; she clung to fastidious table manners, which they ridiculed still more. And now and again, something—a smell of flowers or of aromatic wood burning, or the recollection of a song—would cause some strange thing to flash into her memory.

But here she was, an outcast and a fugitive once again, going ever deeper into the forest, on a wet, raw afternoon now rapidly falling towards night. She thought she could make shift, now, to sleep rough, knowing much more about how to manage than when she had first run away; but on the other hand she knew the limitations of wild living. She knew that all the beds of beech-leaves in the forest would now be soaking wet, and that at this time of year there was very little wild food to be found—no berries, no nuts, roots were hard to find, mushrooms not found at all in that kind of country. She had no means of catching any kind of animal or bird. No, even for a skilled woodcraftsman, it was a bad time of year. Her clothes were wet and torn, and she was very tired and hungry, and still had that frightful slavering on her neck, and the chain weighing her down. Altogether it was a poor prospect. And then, she had heard that there were wolves. So it was hardly to be wondered at that she sank down on the ground and cried.

Presently she recollected something. The silver pentagram, which had made Grimfrith call her a witch. The midwife had called it a witch's token, too, and bade her hide it. There was a lady who had given it to her—well, perhaps it would do something, if she tried.

So she clasped both hands over it, on her neck, and wished, but nothing happened. Then she took it from her neck and laid it on the palm of her hand, and fixed her eyes firmly upon it, keeping her gaze steady and her mind on the Lady, and trying to remember what she looked like. And the white reversed pentagram grew larger and larger, and a door opened in the middle of it, and she went through.

"I was wondering when you would come to me," said the Lady. She was just the same, and so was her beautiful house; there were the quiet gentle maidservants, the beautiful dress of sky blue, the food and drink, the warmth and rest. And at the Lady's first touch, the slave-ring had fallen off and disappeared. Ursulet lay back and enjoyed the comfort, the safety, the reassurance.

"So now you have considered, and decided to accept my help?" said the Lady at last.

"Oh, madame, my state is desperate!" said Ursulet simply. It was strange how she slipped back into the convent's manner of speech.

"I know it—and you a princess born. Arthur's heir, and due by right to sit on Arthur's throne. You are not destined to starve in a forest and be eaten by wolves. Many, many people are seeking you, the time is moving, and your crown hovers in the air over your head. But not all seek you for your own good. The man who can win you can win Britain, and many know it. Therefore, my child, let me make sure that you meet with the right man. Will you do as I say? Oh, dear child, I'm not asking you to pledge your fealty to me now. Pledges of fealty are frightening, and I have no wish to frighten you. But I will direct you for your own good. Will you let me?"

"Oh, yes, madame," she sighed.

"Well then—do not go to Camelot or to Avalon. They are held by your enemies. Go south and west—there is a place called Mai-Dun—the Saxons call it Maiden Castle, for they think the name sounds so—but we call it Mai-Dun, the Great Fortress. Go there, and ask for the Lord of Mai-Dun. He will be your helper and protector."

"And how will I get there, madame?"

"Look, I will draw you a map. We are *here*, a good way south of Wimborne, where your convent was. You go farther south again, and cross a river to the westward here, and then, when you are in sight of the sea, you will find a road going west; keep the sea on your left hand, and go always westward, till you reach the town of Dorchester, and there is Mai-Dun. It will take you many days, but there are villages and small settlements along the way, and the folk will help you."

They seemed to be sitting in a garden, with a floor of white sand, and the lady drew in the sand with an ivory rod. "There you will see me again."

"I see," said Ursulet, and pondered the matter. Then she said,

"My kind benefactress—may I ask one question?"

"Ask on."

48

"This token that you gave me—is it really the token of a witch."

The Lady laughed.

"Now, there's a thing to concern yourself with! Why should you be afraid of the name of witch? You told the Saxon, yourself, that you were a witch, and he believed you, and that saved you. Think of it as you please."

"No, but tell me, for I must be sure. Will you swear to me, by God Almighty, and our Lord Jesus Christ, and His Blessed Mother, that there is no witchcraft in this?"

And suddenly it was as if a mirror was broken—for an instant she saw the Lady's face disfigured as with sudden rage and fear, and there was a smell as of hot metal—and then all was gone, lady and house and garden, and Ursulet was sitting alone in the dark wet forest, shaking with fright. She moved her hand, thinking the silver pentagram was still in it, but somehow it was back on her neck, but the slave-ring and chain were gone. Had she perhaps not taken the pentagram off at all? But then how had the slave-ring disappeared? Her first impulse was to snatch the pentagram off her neck and throw it from her—and then she hesitated, and left it.

And now she was in a desperate state indeed, for the forest was dark and terrible, and far off she thought she could hear a wolf.

"Without doubt she is a witch, that Lady," she said to herself, and she fell to praying, the old Latin prayers of the convent.

Then before her through the trees she saw a sight that made her hold her breath. A light began to glimmer, and in the midst of the light walked a unicorn. It was the loveliest thing she had ever seen—like a noble white horse, but both larger and shapelier than any horse, with silver cloven hoofs, and a silver beard like a goat's, and the long tapering horn above the eyes. She had heard of the unicorn— and although this also might be glamoury, it surely could be nothing unholy.

So she raised her hand and traced a great cross in the air, and said aloud.

"O thou creature, in the name of God the Father, God the Son, and God the Holy Ghost—"

And she waited to see if this also would disappear. But it did not. The unicorn came on steadily towards her, stopped, and sank on its knees, laying its head on her lap.

And now such a feeling of security and holy safety surrounded her that she nestled down beside the unicorn, twining her arms round its neck, and fell happily asleep. And no wolves or any evil thing troubled her at all that night.

When she awoke it was full bright morning and the sun was shining as it should shine in the spring. The unicorn was gone, but so were all the terrors of the night, and she could see that she was out of the forest and on the edge of open country, with villages in sight and a clear road. But she pondered carefully over the visions of the past night.

"One thing is certain," she said to herself, "whatever else I do, I must not go where that witch lady told me. I will *not* go to the Lord of Mai-Dun—but I'll remember his name. That road, there, leads south towards the sea, as she said—but from here I can see a turning that goes back north again. That is the way I will take."

And so she went boldly down into the valley, with her eyes on the far-off church tower, where surely she would find people and help.

NINE

❦

The Snake-Stone

CLOSE to the convent walls of Amesbury, there was a little enclosure of stone walls; inside was fifty feet or so of well-kept grass, with a bed of herbs and a few early spring flowers showing, and a neat stone cell with a chimney. Here, sitting on a bench in the sunshine of a March morning, Ambris found Melior, and an old man sitting beside him.

Melior was a man of fifty, but looked much older; he wore a long white robe, and a white hood over his head, to which was pinned a burnished copper jewel, representing three bars of light coming down from above. His companion, who wore a monk's habit, was a big, muscular man, but bent and slouched with age and infirmity—in his youth he must have been powerful, almost a giant. He turned blank white eyeballs towards Ambris as he heard him come through the wicket-gate, and groped towards him as soon as he heard his voice greeting Melior.

"Oh, I know you, young knight. Come here, stand still and let me feel you."

"Don't be afraid," Melior said aside to Ambris. "Let him feel your face. He is blind."

Ambris stood still, though he shuddered—it was eerie to feel the blind man's fingers running over every inch of his hair, his face, his neck, his breast, his arms.

"Good, good," the blind man muttered. "He's a good lad. I know him—this is the son of the young Gawain and Vivian, as was destined. Young man, the last sight my eyes saw upon earth was when Merlin raised those two from the dead."

Ambris felt the hair on his neck creep with awe, and turned to Melior.

"Could Merlin raise the dead?" he almost whispered.

"Yes—once, and paid for it with his life. I was there too."

"And was it as he says—my parents?"

"Yes, indeed it was, else you had never been begotten."

The blind man moved away from them, to where a little image of Our Lady stood over by the wall among the flowers, and Ambris heard his deep rumbling voice intoning the "Ave Maris Stella," and then breaking into it, "Lady, Lady—beauty beyond belief. Lady, star of the evening. Lady, star of my eyes—I see thee, always I see thee."

Melior led Ambris into his cell and closed the door.

"That is Sir Bertilak. He was a knight once, though not of the Round Table. As you see, he is stone blind. He was for many years enthralled to Morgan le Fay, and she worked her evil magic on him and changed his shape, many times—horribly. I saw it once."

"What shape did she give him?"

"I will not tell you. It was horrible. But he was also the Green Knight, whom your father Gawain the Younger withstood. Some day the story shall be told. But long ago he was released from Le Fay, and serves Our Lady with great devotion, as you saw—but sometimes he invokes her by strange names—But come, you have an errand to me?"

Briefly, Ambris told his quest.

"Arthur's daughter? Yes, I know there was a daughter, who Merlin said should be the hope of Britain. But I do not know at all where she went, or where she is now. Guinevere spoke of her before she died, but she said she had hidden her from the world, for she did not want her to suffer as she had suffered. By that, I understood the Princess was in a nunnery, but not here in Amesbury. The Queen would not tell me more—I think she was unwilling to have her discovered."

"Yes, but reverend sir," said Ambris, "the country needs her. Britain is divided up and torn into pieces—every baron sets up as king, and there is no law, and Mordred is the worst of all. Britain needs its lawful Queen."

"I know, young sir, I know, and therefore we must try to find her."

"Were you the Queen's confessor, reverend sir?"

"I? Why no, I am not a priest—and yet I am a priest. I am a Druid, as Merlin was."

He was silent for a moment, and then said,

"See here, young knight. I will try if we can find where the Princess is, by Merlin's own craft." He began to move back stools and tables so as to clear the floor of the cell, and then drew a circle on the floor with chalk.

"What would you do? Are you going to raise the spirit of Guinevere to tell us?"

"God forbid. I will not draw back the spirit of that poor lady from the peace she has found. No, I will look in the Snake-stone, and see what it can tell us."

From a little casket that stood in a niche of the wall, he brought out a jewel of transparent crystal, like a reliquary.

"Look—this is a very precious thing, and more precious to Bertilak and me than anything but the Body of the Lord. It is a lock of Guinevere's hair."

Ambris looked with reverence into the little round crystal, and saw the hair coiled within—whiter than silver.

"Was her hair always white?"

"After her great sorrow it became white as ashes, and so it was when they clipped this from her head. . . ." He controlled his voice with an effort. "But when she was young it was straw-white, lint-white, with a gleam of sun in it."

He arranged a kind of small altar in the middle of the circle; Bertilak came quietly to the door, seeming to know what was happening, and the two men, with Ambris looking on, made purification with water and fire. Then Melior sat down on a low stool in front of the altar, whereon was the reliquary containing Guinevere's hair, one lighted candle, and a red rose. There was no other light in the room but from the fire on the hearth.

Then, when all was quiet and tranquil, Melior took the Snake-stone from his neck and held it in his right hand. The Snake-stone, which he had been wearing on a thong round his neck, was a perfectly round crystal about the size of a pullet's egg, clear and colourless as water, but with swirling lines of blue and green inside its transparency. Melior looked at it a long time, then reached out and took the reliquary from the altar, and held it in his left hand. After another long wait he raised his left hand with the reliquary to his forehead, and rested it above his eyes. Then he began to speak.

"The child is in a nunnery—a long way from here, but not overseas. Over a river, but not overseas. Mark this, Ambris. Green hills, not wooded—the road passes a giant —a naked giant cut into the chalk of the hill. There is a harbour, a long deep harbour—follow the river up, up towards its source. The winding bourn—I have it—wim . . . wim . . . yes, wim . . . bourn . . . Wimborne. That was the place."

He looked up from the Snake-stone.

"Wimborne in Dorset. I have heard of it. There was a nunnery there, but that's years ago. It could be there still—Come, we must make an ending." And he and Bertilak very carefully and deliberately finished the rite for consulting the Snake-stone, and put everything away, and opened the cell door to let the daylight in. Only when everything was completed did Melior address Ambris again.

"So, my young good knight, I advise you to go to Wimborne, and enquire for the nunnery there. There is a road that passes the naked giant at Cerne—the people there think it is devilish, but I know it is harmless now. Thence turn inland again, and go by Wool and Wareham, and so you come to Wimborne."

"Shall I find her still there?" asked Ambris.

"Who can tell, after these years? But at least it is the first link of the chain. Go on your way, and God speed your search."

TEN

The Pentagram

HE had passed the naked giant, and traced his way up through Wool and Wareham, and now came where Wimborne should be. But no sign of habitation greeted him as he came over the high downs and into the valley. Mounds of brambles and nettles here and there, and broken walls, as if cottages and farms might have stood there—nothing else. No town at the crossing of the little river—a few tumbled stones that might once have been a bridge, otherwise only a neglected ford where his horse stumbled through. There was the outline of a tower standing up against the sky, by which he knew it must be the place; but the tower was crumbling and ruinous. There were the remains of a cobbled street, overgrown with grass, where his horse's hoofs broke the eerie silence—burnt-out houses lay to right and left of him. There was the convent gateway still standing, but no gate. He rode slowly in. The place was a burnt-out ruin, overgrown with many years' weeds. Here and there a wall or a pillar showed where buildings had stood. The church lifted its blackened walls, and the tottering tower leaned over the deserted scene. There was a thick bush of brambles close to where he stood—a bunch of rotting rags fluttered from it. It drew his eye, and as he peered into the bush the eyeholes of a skull peered back at him. . . .

He turned his horse and clattered noisily out of the ruined gateway—down the ghostly road, through the ford —away from that frightful place.

Beyond doubt the Saxons had been there. Been and gone, leaving their horrible signature behind. So that was where the end had been? This was all? Here the trail ran out?

He sat still on his horse and tried to think. Of course, the Saxons had raided here, as they so often did with no one to stop them now. The nunnery had been burnt to the ground, and all the nuns and their pupils had been killed.

So she had been killed too, and there was an end of it. He could go back now and tell that to Lynett and old Bedivere, and watch their faces as their hearts broke. As his was breaking.

Yet some kind of ridiculous optimism made him refuse to admit defeat. Supposing, just supposing, she had escaped? She wouldn't have been a baby. It was hard to tell just when the destruction had happened, but she surely would have been old enough to make a run for it—just supposing? Well, then, which way? Which way more likely than the way he himself had run, straight along the road over the ford—there had been a bridge then. Due south. Well, one road was as good as another to him now—he might as well go on and see if there was any place where a fugitive might have been harboured. He shook his reins, turned the horse away from the ruins of Wimborne, and went south.

Plodding onward straight before him, he found himself first in thick woods, and there made a small camp-fire and spent the night. He slept as best he might, and in the moment of waking he thought he saw a man he knew was Merlin, who said,

"Beware of *this*—but trust *this*."

The first "this" was a pentagram with two points upward and one downward; the second "this" was also a pentagram, but with one point upward. He remembered how his mother (who knew more than anyone might think about magic) had told him that the "right" pentagram was the one with the point upward.

Pondering over this, he was quenching the ashes of his fire, when his eye was caught by a metallic gleam on the ground. There lay a little silver pentagram. But which way up is a pentagram when it is lying on the ground?

He considered it a long time, and then he picked it up and examined it carefully. It was made with loops at the back of each point, so that it could be worn any way— either hanging from one point or from two; and there was nothing to show which way it had last been worn.

He found a piece of thin leather thonging among his things, and attached the pentagram carefully by one point, and hung it about his neck. And the thought occurred to him that this might be a sign that his quest was not quite so hopeless.

❦

ELEVEN

The Gold Cross

FOLLOWING the same road, about noon he smelt woodsmoke, and came to a clearing. There were huts and byres, a couple of cows, and a smoking chimney; and a rough-looking man was sitting on a log and fondling a fat girl with long plaits. The man would be a Jute, Ambris supposed.

"Give you greeting, neighbour," he called, dismounting from his horse. "Can you give me a cup of milk, and perhaps a bite of bread? I've money to pay you."

"Huh?" Burl, for of course it was he, shoved the girl off his lap. "Money? See it?"

Very cautiously Ambris let him see the glint of a silver piece between his finger and thumb.

That seemed to be the extent of the man's vocabulary in the Celtic, but Ambris had learnt a little of the Saxon, which was always useful, and so he turned over to it.

"Good money here—and thanks."

"Go fetch bread and milk," Burl ordered the girl. She slouched off towards the byre. Ambris tried to engage Burl in conversation, which was far from easy in any language.

"You are a Jute, good man?"

"Jute, yes. Jutes good—Angles not so good. Britons bad. Romans bad."

"Saxons?"

"Saxons—some good, some—pah!" He spat.

"You have Saxons here?"

"Yes, yes—Grimfrith, my neighbour."

"But others who come to raid?"

"Yes, yes—six, seven years ago. Very bad. Come up from Poole, over there."

"Was it the Saxons that burnt Wimborne?"

"Ja, ja—those Saxons, they burnt Wimborne. But not my friend Grimfrith. He good man—Christian, I think."

At this moment the girl came back with the milk and bread, and with her were Hertha and the midwife. Hertha no longer required the midwife professionally, but liked her occasional company, and found her a rich source of gossip. They greeted the stranger rather more pleasantly than Burl had done.

"He's asking about those damned Saxon raiders," said Burl.

"Did any escape from Wimborne?" Ambris asked.

"Not a soul," asserted Burl. "Killed the lot, they did—nuns, priests, monks, singing-boys, little girls, babies, old beldames—the lot. Burnt the whole place to the ground. No one escapes from the Saxons."

"Eh?" said the midwife, looking up sideways like a shabby old bird. "You forget your maid—that girl Urz'l. She escaped from the Saxons at Wimborne, she said."

"Oh, did she so?" said Burl. "I'd forgotten."

Ambris's heart gave a leap.

"What was it you called her?"

"Urz'l."

"She escaped from the Saxons, and came here? And where is she now?"

"Oh, devil take her," said Burl. "I sold her two moons ago. She wasn't any use. She was mad."

Desperately anxious to find out what the man was saying, Ambris found that it was beyond his capacity to understand his thick Saxon speech. But the midwife translated.

She said in Celtic, "He says he sold her two moons ago, because she was mad."

Ambris gave a groan of despair.

"Ask him who he sold her to, and where."

The midwife turned to Burl.

"The young lord seems mighty concerned about her. He wants to know who you sold her to."

A look of cunning came into Burl's small eyes. Ambris knew well enough what it meant. Again he showed a coin between finger and thumb, this time a gold one.

Burl roared with laughter. "Here's a to-do about an ugly bony slave! Well, tell him I sold her to Grimfrith the Saxon, over at Grim's Ley. That madwoman! I'll die of laughing!"

"What does he say, good woman?" Ambris pressed the money into Burl's hand, and Burl went on whooping with laughter.

"He says he sold her to Grimfrith the Saxon, at Grim's Ley, which is west from here along the river."

"Thanks, thanks—but why do they laugh?" (For Hertha and the girl had joined in the roaring.)

"They laugh, my lord, because that madwoman said she was a Princess, the daughter of King Arthur and his Queen."

It took Ambris all of that day and most of the next, beating up and down the forest, to find Grim's Ley and the dwelling of Grimfrith. And when he found it, he thought it best to approach it with care. Jutes were all very well; they had been living peaceably under King Arthur for some while, and only wanted to be left alone in their mucky little farmsteads; but Saxons were always out for a fight, even when they were settlers and not raiders. They had seized their lands by violence, and held them by violence; they begrudged the time spent in cultivating them, leaving it to the women as much as they could, and regarding warfare as the only proper occupation for a man.

There was no one outside the house, so Ambris dismounted, hitched his horse, and walked up to the door. He paused a minute, and then knocked.

Instantly the door burst open, and Grimfrith hurled himself out, red-faced, dishevelled and drunk. Giving Ambris no time to state his business, he whirled a club over Ambris's head, shouting, "Damned Welshman!"

Ambris caught his wrist, and the shock made the Saxon drop the club; but he grappled with Ambris now, and they reeled all over the yard together, struggling furiously.

Ambris tried to make him listen.

"You fool, I'm a friend—you fool, stop it—you fool, I want to ask you—" To try and remember the Saxon words while struggling for one's life was just too much. But Ambris had a great deal more science than his adversary, and was also sober; so in a few minutes the Saxon's arm was twisted painfully behind him, and Ambris was holding him firmly down.

"Now—listen," said Ambris in such Saxon as he could muster, "you are a fool. I am a friend. I will give you money if you will tell me a thing."

"Eh?" said the man. "Why the devil didn't you say so before?"

He relaxed, and very cautiously Ambris let him go. The Saxon staggered back against the wall of his hut.

"Well?" he said. "Give me the money."

"First the question," said Ambris. "Where is your slave-girl?"

"Oh—" the man shrugged his shoulders. "Which one?"

"She you—bought—from Burl." (Yes, he had just enough words to get that across.)

"Oh, her! I sent her away—she was a witch. You understand—a witch."

"A witch! Oh, great heavens, not a witch!"

"She wore the witch's sign."

"Where did she go?"

"How the devil do I know? Witches are dangerous. I sent her away. She ran into the woods, I think. Perhaps the wolves ate her."

"But which way did she go?"

"Which way? Any way. I don't know. Why do you want her? Are you a witch too?"

"Oh, take your money," said Ambris, altogether disheartened. He tossed the man a gold piece, and mounted his horse.

For many days he ranged round about the woods, searching every corner, pushing long sticks into every drift of leaves, hoping and yet dreading to find something that would tell him of her fate. In particular he tried to find the spot where he had picked up the silver pentagram, but he could not be sure of it—in any case he found nothing anywhere. At last, having convinced himself that he had done all that was humanly possible, and that this time the trail had indeed run out, he turned back. But first he thought he would look once more at the ruins of Wimborne. Not that he hoped to find any further clue there, but that a kind of fascination drew him back. At least it might be a suitable place to say a prayer for her soul.

So he rode up the deserted street, and tethered his horse at the wrecked gateway, and walked once more among the tumbled blocks of stone, the charred beams, the heaps of weeds, now bursting into green growth. There were wild flowers now, pushing up through the decay. The poor little bones in the corners would have their maiden garlands.

Under a bush a gleam of metal caught his eye—a little gold cross was hanging low down on the bush. He stooped down and put out his hand to take it—and at the same instant another hand, smaller than his but browner, reached out to it from the other side of the bush. Amazed, he drew back and stood up—to find himself looking into the light-grey eyes of a girl.

She stood facing him, almost the same height, thin and brown, with dusty, tangled, straw-coloured hair streaming round her face. She was as lean and tough as a young colt. And she, for her part, was looking up at a well-shaped face, the eyes green, the hair dark chestnut and cut straight across the brow, the mouth boyish and impulsive.

She gasped.

"That's mine. Don't you dare take it. My father gave it me."

Without quite knowing why, he said, "Who was your father?"

"My father was Arthur, King of Britain," she answered.

To her astonishment, the strange young man cried out, and running to her side of the bush, fell at her feet, and kissed the hem of her ragged garment.

"You are the Princess," he said. "Oh, take your father's jewel from my hands," and he held the little gold cross up to her. She almost snatched it from him.

"Who are you, and what do you want?" she said.

"I'm a knight of King Arthur—I'm Ambris, son of Gawain—that is, I'm Sir Ambrosius—" he found himself stammering and blundering. "But what I want—I mean—I want to make you Queen. Many of us do. I've been sent to find you—but we couldn't find you—till now."

For a moment she stood as if minded to accept him; then a suspicious look came over her face, and she skipped quickly back out of his reach. As she moved, he noticed how light and shapely her feet were, and how gracefully her legs moved under the sackcloth garment.

"How do I know I can trust you?" she said. "Who sent you?"

"Sir Bedivere sent me, he who last saw Arthur—and my aunt the Lady Lynett, and Melior, the follower of Merlin—"

She shook her head. He could see that his Princess had turned out to be a very wild bird, who would fly from him if she could. He must not lose her now. So, with a little bit of woodman's cunning, he took care to edge her, as she moved backwards away from him, into a corner of the ruins.

"I still don't know if I can trust you. I was warned that men would seek me out because I was the heiress, and that they would wish me harm."

"Who warned you, and against whom, then?"

"The Abbess warned me, oh, many years ago. She warned me against Mordred, my father's son."

"I know," agreed Ambris. "Mordred is my enemy."

"But I was warned that there were others—I was told to trust none but the Lord of Mai-Dun."

"But the Lord of Mai-Dun *is* Mordred."

This was a shock to her.

"Who told you to trust the Lord of Mai-Dun?" Ambris continued.

"Oh, the Lady—a Lady I met in the wood."

"Did she give you any token?"

"Yes, she gave me—Ah!—as she caught sight of the charm on Ambris's neck. "She gave me *that*—but you're wearing it upside down—"

"I'm wearing it the right way up," said Ambris. "The other way is the sign of a witch. I fear your Lady was a witch, and I think I know her."

"Oh—" Ursulet looked to and fro wildly. "Now I don't know whom to trust, or where I stand. First I'm to beware of Mordred, and trust the Lord of Mai-Dun—and then the Lord of Mai-Dun *is* Mordred—then the Lady is a witch, and all she told me must be false—and you wear the witch's star, but it's reversed and you say it's not the witch's star—and as for you, I don't know you—Oh, let me go!" She tried to run past him, but he had her in a corner, and she would not come within an arm's reach of him. "Oh, let me go back to begging at the farms. At least when they set the dogs on me I know what they mean."

"Oh, please, please," he exclaimed, driven to exasperation, "don't be such a *silly* lady!"

She gasped, and then a smile relaxed the corners of her mouth. This couldn't be the speech of a deceiver. "Why," she said to herself, "he's nothing but a boy. Just a young boy—he could be younger than I am."

"I think I will trust you," she said, and put out her brown hand to him. He took it in his own, and lifted it to his lips, which made her give a little "Oh!" of surprise.

"Where will you take me?" she said.

"I think we will go first to Shaston—it's not far, and

there's a nunnery there, where you can be refreshed and rested, and dressed as you ought to be."

So he led her out of the ruins, and mounted his horse, and showed her how to get up behind him—she had ridden pillion far back in her childhood, but almost too far back to remember. And when she clasped her arms round his body, he was astonished at the way his heart beat, and kept his face sternly forward so that she could not see how it reddened.

TWELVE

❧❧ ❧❧

A Royal Progress

At Shaston, he told the nuns that this was a noble lady who had been held prisoner by the Jutes and Saxons, and that he was taking her home to her kindred, but for the present he must not tell her name.

To Ursulet, it felt like slipping back into a familiar world long lost, and the nuns were quick to notice that though she looked so wild, she had the convent manners, that came back to her as she looked around her. They bathed her, long and luxuriously, and rubbed her poor weary body with healing oils, exclaiming over the welts and scars left by six years of beating. They washed her hair, and combed it out, and braided it into two long plaits. The Abbess had a treasure-chest of her own, where were kept the beautiful dresses that the professed nuns had worn, once only, on the day when each one became the Bride of the Lord. Out of these she picked the best one, which was her own—a lovely white gown, made in a fashion of twenty years past, all embroidered with gold and colours; and the nuns arrayed Ursulet in this. So, from a dishevelled bundle of hay and sacking, she stepped out in her full royalty, tall, white-robed, glimmering, flaxen-haired and grey-eyed—Guinevere's daughter.

Ambris saw her, coming slowly down the broad stairway into the refectory—and he fell on his knees before her.

"O my Lady!" he said. "You lack nothing now but a royal crown of gold—and that, I swear I will win for you."

They rested at Shaston for a week, and then set out for Avalon. The nuns provided Ursulet with a neat dress of dark blue wool, and a cloak and hood of the same, and boots of the finest soft leather. They would have given her a palfrey, but Ursulet could not ride. She could milk goats and cows, and was unafraid of a bull or a buck goat, but saddle-horses had never come her way. So she was content to ride pillion behind Ambris, and he was more than content. It seemed to him, as they set out on a fine April morning, with everything bursting into bloom around them, that his cup of joy was full and running over. He was bringing home his Princess—and what a Princess! And there she rode behind him, pressed close against his back, her arms clasped tight around his waist, her soft sunburnt cheek, like a ripening peach, almost touching his as they rode. . . .

Their way from Shaston to Avalon should not have been far, and it led mostly up over dry ridgeways, grassy and warm in the spring sunshine. They rested at noon on a green hillside, with the larks singing above them. Nothing could have been fairer or happier. In the valleys below them the endless bushland of hawthorn was still all shadowy grey twigs, but a haze of green was spreading upon it, and in places there were banks of blackthorn showing drifts of snow-white blossoms.

Yet, as they rode, there grew upon Ambris an uneasy sense as of eyes watching. Nothing to see, but. . . . He began glancing over his shoulder, but saw nothing—yet. Ursulet noticed this, and glanced back too—and he felt her shudder.

"What is it, lady?" he asked. "Did you see anything behind us?"

"No—nothing behind us. I wondered if you did—Only—something made me shiver. They say it's when a man walks over your grave." She laughed nervously.

"Come, we'll go faster. Hold tight." They galloped for a bit, and in the excitement lost the fear; but when Ambris slackened the pace and let his horse walk, there was that sense again of someone watching, someone following. They were passing through dry heathy country, golden with gorse, and they went down into a dell; at the bottom of the dell he looked back, and could have sworn that a head moved on the lip of the dell above him. He looked to right and left, and almost thought he saw another at each side. He said nothing, but shook the reins and spurred his horse up the slope, and then looked round and over the border of the dell. Nothing—only open heath and gorse as far as the eye could see. But a noise began, a strange disturbing noise. Too early in the year for grasshoppers or crickets, surely? A noise like crackling, like whispering, like laughing. Not pleasant laughter, either. He wondered if Ursulet heard it, but would not ask her. But she put her lips close to his ear, and said, "Do you hear it?"

"I do indeed."

"What is it?"

"God knows. But as God knows, I trust He won't let it hurt us. We must go on."

They went on, but as they went the watchers, whatever they were, grew bolder and more insistent. The chattering grew louder. No shapes could be seen yet, but tufts of heather moved, and gorsebushes shook, and not with the wind.

Now they left the high heath country, and began to go down into woodlands. The road was no more than a beaten track, but it was as much as men expected in those parts where the Roman roads were no longer kept up, or where they had not been. This was at least the indication of a plain way to go; and it led downwards, and abruptly plunged into the shade of the untouched forest. The great oaks stood as they had stood from the beginning; and the undergrowth closed up to the track, keeping its secrets.

Undoubtedly there were things that tracked them, that parted the leaves and looked and were gone.

There were side-turnings out of the track here and there, but it seemed obvious that the way was straight on. But presently for no apparent reason, Ambris's horse stopped short in its tracks, and stood shivering. At the same moment, Ambris felt a tremor run over him—not so much cold, as a disturbing vibration—his hair stood on end, something oppressed his breathing. He clenched his hands to try and stop the tremor. He could see on his horse's neck the sweat breaking out. The horse backed, shaking its head from side to side, its nostrils flaring, the whites of its eyes showing.

"We can't go on," said Ambris over his shoulder.

"I know," she answered. "I can feel it. No, we can't go on. We must go another way."

He turned the horse—the frightening sensation ceased, and the horse was calmer. But as he turned, he glimpsed the strange things in the undergrowth behind him. They gave before him as he turned, and closed in behind. He retraced his steps, and found a side track that promised to lead round and rejoin their road; he took it, but after about a mile it was the same—something forced him to turn. And then again, and again. The unknown things were driving him as a dog drives sheep. The sun began to decline, and the colours of the forest to deepen—and he began to see

66

the creatures. He would not have mentioned them to Ursulet, but she spoke first.

"Did you see what I saw?"

"What was it?"

"A man's head—but it hadn't a body to it. Just a head, and it rolled along like a ball. Did you see it?"

"Yes, and I saw a little dwarfish black man with horns."

"Worse than that—there was one like a child running on all fours, but its four legs were six."

"There was one like a bird, on long legs with a long neck—but it had a man's face on its long neck."

"Oh, Ambris, I don't like them a bit, not a bit!"

"Nor do I, my darling." (In his fear he had no consciousness of calling her that.) "I'll get you out of here as soon as I can."

"I know you will. Should we pray, do you think? I've prayed inwardly, but should we pray aloud?"

"Yes, let us do that." So they halted, and together said the Pater and Ave. The things seemed to give back a little, but were still there. Then Ambris remembered something of what his mother had taught him about pentagrams, and made the pentagram of the Right Way on all four sides of them. Again the things took a few paces back. But when Ambris moved his horse on again, the things still followed them, though further off. Ambris had no idea of the way now—he simply had to go as the things sent him. Holding the reins in his left hand, he clasped his right hand firmly over Ursulet's two hands, which were cold and tremulous. Turning his head over his shoulder, he laid his cheek against hers, without thinking at all. "My dearest," he said, and she made a little sighing noise in reply, and pressed herself hard against his back. He could feel her trembling, and hear how her teeth chattered. And there was nothing he could do but go on, and try not to look round at the things.

The forest was dark now, almost too dark for the horse to see its way—and then at last there was a light, and Ambris and Ursulet both cried out together. A light, and from an open door! It had loomed up upon them before they could see it through the trees—a tall house or castle set upon a hillside, with a causeway over a deep foss, where they were already going—a courtyard over the causeway, and a door standing open.

"Oh, thank God, thank God!"

❦ ❧

THIRTEEN

To Dance at Whose Wedding?

THEY rode in, and as if they had been expected, serving-men ran out, and women too, hospitable voices bade them come in, willing hands helped them to dismount; grooms led the horse away, and they found themselves in the midst of human concern and comfort. This was no palace of glamour, but a good earthly dwelling of men.

A tall man in a leather jerkin, who seemed to be in command, poured out a cup of good ale for each of them.

"The master bids you welcome," he said. "There are rooms provided for you—go and rest till it is time for dinner."

A quiet maidservant took charge of Ursulet and led her away up a wooden stair to a soler room, above the hall. As the maid hung up Ursulet's cloak and took off her gown, to dress her, as the custom was, in a robe kept in the house for guests, Ursulet asked her,

"What is this castle called?"

"Maiden Castle," the girl replied.

"Maiden Castle!" Ursulet's head whirled. "But we *can't* have come that far out of our road. Maiden Castle's far in the south, by Dorchester—"

"Oh, but this is the new one," said the girl. "Mai-Dun Newton, they call it. My lord finished building it last year."

"And—who is your lord?" asked Ursulet, her voice faltering. She knew the answer before it was given.

"The Earl Mordred, to be sure, madam."

"Then I must go!" cried Ursulet wildly. "Give me my cloak again—send word to my knight—I'll not stop here—"

The girl—tall and strong, with muscles that could have held Ursulet down, and a sly mouth and eyes—stood over her as if she had been a raving fever patient.

"Now, now, now, my lady—what's this? No, I'll not give you your cloak to go rushing off again. Have no fear of my Lord Mordred. He's a courteous gentleman, be sure, and wishes you nothing but good."

Ursulet sat helplessly down. It seemed it was no use to fight or try to run.

"Well—and who is the lady of the castle, then?"

"The lady of the castle—Well. . . ." The girl turned away and busied herself folding Ursulet's riding dress. "Well, at present it's my lady Aestruda—but foot the dance well, my lady, and it might be you."

"What do you mean?"

But the maid did not answer; she only said,

"What pretty hair you have, my lady. Come, I'll comb and braid it for you."

Presently she descended by long winding stairs into the great hall. It was many years since Ursulet had known a lordly hall, but some recollection came dimly back to her now. Yes, thus it was—the vast space, rafters above and rushes below, lit by the flickering light of a great central fire; the long tables, without cloths, running down the sides, where the men-at-arms sat; the dais at the far end, with the high table draped with rich cloths and backed with tapestry. And here she found herself face to face with Mordred.

He stood before her, thick legs astride, arms akimbo; a heavily built man, red-faced, coarse-grained; not yet forty, but with his face reddened with drinking and pouches below his blue protuberant eyes. His hair, blond and inclining to red, was cut square across his brows and fell to his shoulders, and a heavy moustache hung down in the Saxon style over bad-tempered lips. But he was smiling.

"My lady Ursulet," he said, and she was surprised that he knew her name, "you are heartily welcome here, by the Mass! You'll be my guest here for a while. Come, sit you down. Serve up the food, you scullions."

She looked round anxiously for Ambris, and was relieved to see him some little distance off, towards one end of the high table. They exchanged glances, but neither of them happy ones.

"Here, meet my two sons," said Mordred, and two youths came forward. "This is Morcar, my eldest." There was a ring of pride in his voice. "He's as tough a fighter for his sixteen years as you'll find, fears neither man nor devil, and has a dozen bastards about the bailey—hain't you, my big brat?" and he slapped him on the shoulder. Morcar was as tall as his father, a handsome boy with the bold blue eyes of Arthur's race, and a swaggering walk. He kissed Ursulet's hand, and ran his eyes over her as if she had been merchandise for sale.

"And this is Morwen." There was no attempt to disguise the coldness in Mordred's voice. The boy was about fifteen, his features irregular and without grace—brown eyes looked up at Ursulet, deprecating; he bit his lip and reddened, and kissed her hand quickly and backed away. "Poor chap," Mordred commented. "You must excuse him. I don't know what use he is. Not like this one," and he drew Morcar forward to sit at Ursulet's left hand, she being on Mordred's left. Morwen was left to find himself a place at the end of the table; he found himself next to Ambris, who cleared a place for him.

Ursulet's recollection of feasts in the high hall, and of course in the refectory, was that they always began with grace; but no grace was said here. Everyone fell to as soon as the dishes were on the table, or even before; and the noise and riot were appalling. On Mordred's right hand was a lady in a bright yellow gown, very bold and brassy, who drank a great deal and talked very loudly; Ursulet supposed this must be the Lady Aestruda. Behind her chair stood an elderly woman in attendance, dressed in black silk and veiled almost to the eyes. Ursulet wondered what the waiting-maid had meant by her hint that she herself might be the lady of the castle. She had no wish to be the lady of such a castle as this.

Ambris, from where he sat, could see both the sons of Mordred, one beside him, the other at his father's side. A page, offering dishes, stumbled as he handed the dish to Morwen, the younger and brown-eyed one—the page tipped the dish, and a stream of gravy went over Morwen's tunic. Morwen exclaimed, but took a towel from the boy, and without any fuss began to wipe down his own garment. But Morcar, from where he sat, jumped up and was beside him, grabbing the unfortunate page by the ear.

"Look, Morwen, this won't do!" he cried. "This filthy cur's spoilt your jerkin, and by God's body, you sit there and do nothing! Here," and he unhitched a dog-whip from his belt, "whip the knave. Come on."

Morwen shook his head, and made no move to take the whip.

"Come on, I say—father, he must whip him, must he not? Morwen, you're a pale-faced dastard. Here, take the whip," and he thrust it into Morwen's hand and, holding his hand, tried to make him whip the boy. Morwen wrenched his hand away, so Morcar turned away from him, and slashed the page across the face—left, right, left, right—The page backed away from the table, into the middle of the room, Morcar following him. The rest of the company looked on, laughing and applauding. Mordred turned to Ursulet. "That's my brave boy," he said. "The other's a milksop."

Ursulet watched in horror as the page was driven backwards, step by step, towards the fire. Morcar was lashing and lashing and lashing, as if unable to stop himself.

Then Ambris sprang from his place, overturning his chair, and jumped from the dais, reaching a long arm out between the page and the fire just in time to catch him back. Morcar's whip fell on Ambris's knuckles, but the company stopped shouting, and waited. Morcar, his face working with rage, lifted his whip again, this time towards Ambris. In the hush, Ursulet made her voice heard.

"My lord earl—we are your guests."

"Oh, true, true," grumbled Mordred, subsiding. "All right, Morcar, my boy, let them go. Sit down."

Ambris turned and made formal obeisance.

"I beg pardon, my lord earl—I supposed that you did not wish to see murder done."

"Oh, go on, go on. Give us some more ale."

Later, the hall was cleared, and Ursulet wondered if it was for dancing. She dimly remembered such a thing, when she was very little—for things of that kind, long forgotten, began to come back to her now.

But it seemed it was not for dancing, though the men-at-arms carefully cleared a space, and trumpets were sounded —there entered no mummers, but a priest in his vestments with two acolytes. Gravely, and as far as he was able gracefully, Mordred offered Ursulet his arm, as if indeed for dancing, and led her down till she stood in front of the priest, and Morcar closed up on Mordred's other side. Then the priest began his Latin, and Ursulet listened in astonishment. She was familiar enough with the Mass, though she had not heard it now for six years; but this was no office she had ever heard before. And suddenly it dawned on her —this was a marriage! She was being wedded to Morcar, without any consent of hers.

Mordred stepped back and drew Ursulet and Morcar together, and the priest broke into the vernacular.

"Dost thou, Morcar, take this woman Ursulet, to be thy wedded wife?"

"I do," said the handsome sulky boy, and put out his hand, but Ursulet kept her hand behind her back.

"Dost thou, Ursulet, take this man—"

"No!" cried Ursulet. "No!" she shrieked as loudly as she had breath in her body. "No!" she shrieked again, and heard it echo back from the rafters, while all around her confusion broke out.

Mordred took her arms firmly.

"Dear girl, don't be foolish. I know this is a surprise to you, but what the devil—you must have a husband, and where's a better than my young Morcar?"

"I won't," said Ursulet, gritting her teeth.

"Oh, come—won't's a bad word for a young lady to use. I think we may make you change your mind. Think—you will be Queen of Britain when Morcar is King—"

"I *am* Queen of Britain!" she said, with such force of conviction that the priest, a red-faced stupid man, looked up in surprise.

"My dear, I think you had better not be obstinate," said Mordred, and she felt his nails begin to bite into her arm. She looked round wildly for Ambris—he was not there. Shaking off Mordred's arm, she took a step towards the priest and threw herself into his arms.

"Oh, sir priest—I beg you, I beg you—don't wed me to this man!"

"And why not, my daughter?"

"Because—because—" Suddenly she saw where a white lie—well, a bluff—might help her. "Because I am married already. Sir Ambrosius and I were wedded three days ago at the convent at Shaston."

A buzz of astonishment broke out.

"Is that so?" said the priest, rather slowly comprehending. "In that case—why—why, my lord earl, the lady says she's married already."

"Oh, hell blast the stupid woman!" exclaimed young Morcar, grinding his heel into the rushes. "Father said I

72

was to take her, and she's fair enough, and I'd have bedded her too—and now I'm made a fool of!"

"Is this true?" Mordred glowered over Ursulet.

"Yes, my lord," said she, shrinking in terror from his furious face.

"My lord earl," said the priest, "it would seem that it would be—well, doubtful—to marry her to the Lord Morcar at present. It would be better to wait."

All drew back from Ursulet, and Morcar stumped away. Mordred made no move toward her, and the priest steadied her with his hand. She felt she had at least gained a breathing space.

"Oh, let it be, let it be, then!" Mordred exclaimed. "All right, girl, you can go to your chamber. No wedding tonight." The company groaned with disappointment. "But you can all drink just as well without a wedding." They cheered once more. Ursulet turned away gladly, looking for her maid. She wondered again where Ambris was, and whether all was well with him. But as she went, over her shoulder she heard Mordred say to the priest, "As for you, Sir John, don't leave the castle yet. Stay within call. I might need you very soon to re-marry a new-made widow."

And then she understood what a deadly peril she had brought upon Ambris.

❦ ❧

FOURTEEN

A Dark Old Woman

AMBRIS, as the commotion subsided that followed his rescue of the page, felt his arm seized, and found himself being drawn into one of the wall-recesses that surrounded the main hall. Young Morwen had hold of his hand and seemed unwilling to let it go. The boy looked very young, and his eyes were full of tears that he fought to keep back.

"Oh, sir knight!" he exclaimed, "I want to thank you—oh, you don't know what it means to me. Look, that's the first act of mercy and kindness I've ever seen done in this place." He turned his head awkwardly aside, for the tears had spilled over. Ambris avoided looking at him.

"Sir," the boy went on, "it's frightful for me here. You don't think, do you, that a man *has* to be a brute, like—like my brother and my father?"

"Surely not," said Ambris, but felt embarrassed. "Look, anything I can do to help you—"

"I must go," said the boy, listening like a nervous dog. "If Morcar finds me, he'll put the knotted string round my head . . ." and he was gone.

Ambris stood in doubt, and was about to turn to go back to the hall. There was noise and commotion going on, and he felt it was no place for Ursulet. But before he could turn, he felt a tug on his arm. He looked down, and there was the most repulsive little old woman he had ever seen. She was bent two-double, and hobbled sideways; a ragged mud-coloured cloak covered her, from which came a daunting smell of age, misery and neglect. Her mouth was a black toothless hole.

He recoiled from her, but she kept her hold on his sleeve.

"Young knight," she mumbled, "if you value your lady's life, come with me."

"What?" He drew back shuddering.

"No questions. Your own life isn't worth a straw at this moment, and hers is in worse case. Come, at once and quietly."

Nothing could be worse than going back to the hall, he felt, so, with his hand on his dagger, he followed her. She led him to a door in a dark entry, unlocked it, and went on into deeper darkness still. She took a small lantern from under her robe, and bobbed on before him like a gnome. Down a flight of steps, along a stony echoing passage, where all one side were sinister black cells closed with gratings.

"But these are dungeons!" he exclaimed, and heard his voice echo hollowly. "Why have you brought me here, old woman?"

She stopped, turned, and held the lantern up—she no longer stooped or crouched, but stood up very tall.

"Why, lad, don't you know me yet?" she chuckled.

"Aunt Lynett!"

"The same, my boy." She embraced him warmly. "Oh, I'm sorry for these stinking rags. They are necessary, you see, for the disguise."

He looked at her as she stood in the dim light of the lantern—brown, leathery as ever, her cheeks smeared with soot.

"Oh my dear aunt—" he said. "But for heaven's sake, what have you done to your teeth?"

For where he had been accustomed to see her firm, perfect if slightly prominent teeth, was an unsightly gap.

"Oh, my teeth are well enough," she laughed. "A bit of apothecary's plaster over them, that's all. Under that they're as good as ever, and ready to bite you or any man." Her eyes twinkled, and he felt that she was enjoying her frightful disguise.

"But why am I in the dungeons?"

"Why, better here with me, than here with two of Earl Mordred's men. See, lad—I don't need a magic mirror to know it was only a matter of a minute before Mordred gave his men orders to make away with you. So I thought it was better that I take you out of sight first. He'll not have given orders specially to this man or that man, and none will come back to report to him, so that if any questions are asked afterwards he can take no blame—I know him. So—provided you disappear, each man will think

75

another man did it, and he will just count you—lost. You'll be safe enough where I'll hide you."

"But the Princess?"

"I'll see that she's safe. I go to and fro in the kitchen, you see, and through all the rooms, to do the dirtiest work, and no one thinks of questioning poor Madge the Dishclout." She cackled. "I'll watch the Princess, and in due time we'll make good our escape. But come now, I'll show you your quarters. They're none so bad."

They went down another stair to another deep level, with more dungeons along the gallery; the stonework seemed to be new, as far as Ambris could see in the dim light of the lantern. Then down to a third level; and at the farthest extremity of this, the passage seemed to come to an end; but Lynett went on, and Ambris saw that where a blank wall seemed to be, there was a narrow vertical fissure in the rock, just big enough to squeeze through.

"We're both thin enough," said Lynett. "A fat man couldn't get through this—I doubt if my lord Mordred could." Ambris felt the dread of the deep underground, the fear of being trapped under rocks far from the daylight, gripping him. But Lynett led on for a few steps, and then halted before a solidly made oaken door, which she opened with a key.

Inside was a reasonable little cell—a dungeon no doubt, but a dungeon with some comforts. A little fireplace with a chimney held a small fire of logs. A thin stream of water flowed out from the wall into a stone basin, from which it escaped into a groove cut across the floor and out through a drainage hole. There were candle sconces on the walls, into which Lynett fixed candles and lighted them. There was a bed with pillows and blankets, and a basket containing food.

"You've all you want here," she said. "The smoke from the fire goes into the great kitchen chimney, so it's never noticed, and the water's always clean and good to drink. You can lock the door from the inside, and open only when I knock thus."

"However did such a place come to be?" he asked.

"Oh, it's hard to say, but it seems it was made in the old time—you see, Mordred built his New Mai-Dun on the shell of an older castle—it may even have been made by the Romans, for look, the floor is made of tiles. Mordred and his company don't know of this cell—they only know the upper ones that he made. You should be safe enough here for a day or two. You've plenty of food here, and I'll bring you more every day, and there's firewood and candles. And to save you going melancholy-mad with being alone, look here." She placed in his hands a large, ponderous, handwritten book, a collection of chivalrous romances. "Here's a treasure for you, to pass the time! Now, aren't you glad I taught you your letters, even if I did beat you sometimes? God knows you're slow at reading, but if you sit down and try to worry this out, it'll give you something to do."

"Oh, aunt, you're very kind to me."

"Tush, boy, what else? I prepared this for you some time back."

"You prepared for me—for us? But how did you know we were coming?"

"Oh, where the vultures gather, there the corpse will be found. Morgan le Fay is here—didn't you see her? That woman in black who pretends to be the Lady Aestruda's maid. We learnt she was here—by means we have—and we knew she would fetch you here. Which she did."

"Yes, we were—what could I say?—driven here by Things."

"I know. I've heard tell of them. I never see or feel or hear anything that isn't of this world—now—but others do. They say that Morgan's spells are powerful, and you may yet have to guard against them. But God be with you, and you'll be proof against Morgan and all the lot of them. Rest you now, boy, while I go and watch the Princess."

"You will give her—my regards, and tell her I'm still alive?"

"I'll give her your love, for that's what you mean."

So he shut the door behind her, locking it, and heard its hollow clang and how her footsteps died away down the long passages—and then he was left alone, so terrifyingly alone, down under fathoms upon fathoms of earth in the utter darkness, with his candles and his little fire for his only company.

❦ ❧

FIFTEEN

In Mordred's Power

THE chamber assigned to Ursulet was a pleasant enough room, as she reflected when she woke in the morning. She lay in a fine draped bed, and the walls that surrounded her were hung with tapestry, very gay and colourful. The sunshine came in through narrow windows, high up—and that was the one drawback, she felt. It was impossible to see out, and obviously it would be very difficult to escape. And Ursulet was quite sure that she must escape as soon as possible, but not without Ambris.

The same rather sly maid waited on her, bringing her water for washing and an excellent breakfast; she was attended by a rather dirty old woman, not a very nice creature to have about the place. When they had gone away, Ursulet tried the door, but as she expected found it locked. And not long after, the maid, bobbing obsequiously, ushered in Mordred, and bobbing again, withdrew.

"Madam," he began, "I've come to offer you condolences, and perhaps congratulations."

"What do you mean?"

"Well, condolences on your widowhood, and congratulations on the prospect of a second marriage."

Ursulet closed her eyes and sank back where she sat. A cold faintness swept over her.

"What—what has happened?"

"Why, it's very regrettable, but your husband, the good Sir Ambrosius, has disappeared since last night—no sign of him anywhere—and we fear the worst."

"Murderer!" she cried. "If he's dead, it's you that made away with him."

"I? Why, no, madam. I've laid no hand on him, and that I'll swear. I tell you, I do not know where he is. But the castle is full of staircases, and awkward corners, and deep wells—we fear he is lying at the bottom of some such—"

"You fear? but where *is* he then? Where is his body?"

"My dear lady, I tell you, no one knows."

"Then find his body," she cried, "for until you do, I count myself married to him, and I will *not*—I will *not*—I will *not* marry your son Morcar or anyone else."

"Is that so?" he said in a quiet and considering voice. "Why then, my men shall have orders to search more carefully, and bring his body for you to see. Will that content you?"

"No—yes—no!" she cried wildly, seeing now that she had made his danger, if he were still alive, worse than before. "Oh, whether he's alive or dead, I *won't* marry Morcar."

"Indeed?" She was sitting on the edge of the bed, and he came and sat beside her. "But I can think that you might have reason. Now tell me—you and this Sir Ambrosius—you were not many days together. Did he consummate the marriage?"

She looked at him blankly, not knowing what he meant.

"Oh, God's bones, don't you understand? Did you bed together?"

She blushed deeply. "No, we did not."

"So you're still a maid?"

"Yes, my lord."

"Well then, you still have a treasure you would fain not lose. But supposing you lost it—to me? You'd be glad enough to take Morcar then."

She shrank away from him, but he had both arms firmly round her, and was thrusting her back on the bed.

"Let me go—let me go—you're my brother—my father's son—"

"What of that?" he laughed coarsely. "So was Arthur my mother's brother. It runs in the family. You'd be glad enough to take Morcar to save the scandal."

She tried to push him off, but even her muscular arms were not strong enough.

"If you don't let me go," she cried wildly, "I'll swallow my tongue and choke myself, and die. I know how to, and I will. Then what use will I be to you?" (And this was a desperate bluff, for though she had heard the Jutish midwife speak of such things, she really did not know how it was done.)

He hesitated, and relaxed his hold—and at the moment a loud knocking sounded on the door.

"Oh, devil take it, who's there?"

No answer, but the knocks continued to thunder. He got up from the bed, and Ursulet sprang away into the farthest corner of the room.

"Who's there? Oh, go to hell, whoever you are—"

No word answered him, only the knocking went on, louder and louder.

"Oh, God's blood and death, what in the name of Satan is it?" and he opened the door, and made to close it again. But incredibly quickly, before he could do so, the old serving-woman skipped into the room under his arm, and stood looking stupidly up at him from under her cover of brown rags.

"Beg pardon, my lord, it's only me, come to see to her ladyship's room. Work must be done whether or no, my lord."

"Get out, hag!"

"Oh yes, my lord, when I've done me work. But poor old Madge the Dishclout has her duty to do the same as greater folks, to scrape out the ashes, and empty the washing-water and the—"

"Go to the devil!" Mordred strode past her, banging the door as he went, and turning the key in the lock. The moment he was gone the old woman stood up to twice her apparent height, threw off the dirty cloth from her head, and said in a completely different voice,

"Come quickly—Sir Ambris is waiting for you."

"But how—" Ursulet looked helplessly at the locked door.

"Oh, this way—come on—" and the old woman hustled her through a little door behind the tapestry, and into stony, winding, twisting darkness.

❦ ❧

SIXTEEN

Through Darkness and Water

IN Ambris's refuge, he lost all reckoning of time. He supposed that a day could not have gone by, for Lynett had not revisited him as she said she would, though he had no lack of food and drink in his cell. He saw candles burn down, and replaced them from time to time, and kept his little fire going; and he tried to read a romance, but found it very difficult. At least it tired him, so that he slept. And waking up out of sleep, with a sudden beating of his heart he saw a woman standing before him.

Not Lynett certainly—no, he remembered this one, the white-robed, golden-sandalled woman who had haunted his vigil of knighthood. He jumped up from his straw pallet.

"Oh, lie down again, dear young knight," the woman said in the soft voice he remembered. "You are weary of your own company. What life is this for a young man who should be pursuing the phantom of Beauty?"

He shrank back from her.

"No, have no fear of me, lad. It's not any carnal pleasure I seek with you. I'm a kinswoman of yours on both sides, indeed. I am great-aunt to your mother, and to your father too—for Nimuë and Morgause were both my sisters."

"You must be very old!" he gasped stupidly.

"Old enough as the world goes. As old as the soul of Beauty. Look at me, lad."

Against his will his eyes were drawn to hers—green eyes—his mother's eyes were a clear blue-green, and his own eyes, he knew, were green too, but these were like a cat's, jewel-like, but with the pupils wide, wide and black.

"Look into my eyes—yield yourself to them, fall right into them. For, old as you think me, I am far, far older.

I am she to whom the young men of the East gladly sacrificed their manhood—oh, no, lad, never fear me, I'll not put the moon-shaped sickle into your hand. But give yourself into my hands, and I think the love of one woman will trouble you but little, for you shall know the love of Beauty—not this one nor that one, but the Beautiful that you will never touch or kiss, but follow forever over horizon beyond horizon. Far, far lovelier than any daughter of man—a Grail holier than that which you have called the Holy Grail—terrible and guarded with death and madness, but dear beyond all thought and all dream. I am the White One, of whom all other white ladies are but shadows. Forget all others, and seek the unattainable in the pools of my eyes."

Helpless and spellbound, he drifted towards her as if towards sleep. Then suddenly a knock sounded on the door—Lynett's agreed signal. He broke from the glamour—and like a burst bubble, the lady was gone. Rubbing his eyes, he stumbled across and opened the door—and there found, not Lynett, but young Morwen, big-eyed in the dim light. Ambris cried out, and made to shut the door again, but the boy laid hold of his arm.

"No, don't shut the door on me—it's all right, I'm a friend. The Lady Lynett sent me. Look, here's her token," and he put into Ambris's hand one of the massive silver rings that he knew his aunt wore.

"All right, come in."

"My lord," said the boy, "she sent me to warn you. She is with the Lady Ursulet now. I was to tell you, get ready to go, and quickly, for it will be a near thing. My father thought you had been put away secretly, and that was well, for he didn't search, but the Lady Ursulet bade him show her your body, else she wouldn't marry my brother Morcar. So he is having search made for you."

All this was hard for Ambris to take in, dull as he was with his long confinement.

"To marry Morcar?" he said. "Mordred's son?"

"Yes, my lord. They brought the priest there and all, but she would not marry him, being already married to you."

"What?" The whole cell seemed to reel round Ambris. "She said she was married to *me*?"

"Of course, my lord," said the boy. "You are married to her, are you not?"

"Why—why, yes," he stammered. "Yes, of course we are married."

"And so, of course," said Morwen, "if you were not dead before, my father will make sure you are. Oh, my father's a fell man! Sir—will you let me go with you when you escape? For my father and my brother will kill me."

"Surely," said Ambris, looking down on the lad's earnest, white-rimmed eyes. No more than a child—and he, Ambris, was he so very much older? But certainly he must protect this boy.

"The Lady Lynett says you must put out your fire and all the candles," Morwen said, "and be dressed and shod, and pack provisions for a journey—she herself will bring weapons."

So they quickly made their preparations, but Ambris's head was whirling and his heart singing. Ursulet had said that! Not one recollection remained in his mind of the vision of the White Lady—only of Ursulet, one woman, human and to be loved with a man's love.

As their preparations were complete, Morwen quenched the fire, and put out the candles one by one, till they stood uneasily in complete darkness. They listened, and each thought the other must surely hear his heart beating. So they listened.

Then there were soft steps, and the agreed knock. Ambris opened the door quickly and quietly; there was Lynett, with her horn-lantern, and behind her Ursulet, muffled in a dark cloak.

No time for words of greeting. "Come quickly," said Lynett in a gruff whisper. "They've got the dogs out. The narrow crack will be no protection. Come with me, and stick together now." With ears sharpened by fear, Ambris could hear a tumult of men and dogs coming down the echoing passages. "Not much time," Lynett went on. "Follow me, and do as I say. Don't ask questions."

Lynett leading, Ursulet went next, and Ambris put the boy Morwen in front of him, and brought up the rear. Like a string of blind beggars, they stumbled down the pitch-dark passage, their feet hardly able to keep them on the rough path. The noise was behind them, and ahead all that Ambris could see was the faint glow of Lynett's lantern obscured by those in between. The path went steeply down—they had to steady themselves with their hands against the clammy sides of the passage—and a new sound suddenly came up to them—the rushing of water.

"Now," said Lynett, halting. "There's water here, and there's death behind. If anyone's heart fails them they can stay behind for the dogs and Mordred. Otherwise—let yourselves down into the water—draw a long breath, hold your nose with your fingers, shut your mouth, hold your breath, and go under. Let the water carry you while you count fifty—hold your breath all that time. If you raise your head above the water before that, your brains will be dashed out on the rocks above you. Is that clear? It may be death, but there's certain death behind us."

They could hear the bloodthirsty clamour of the hounds close to them now. The water was at their feet, dimly seen in the lantern's glimmer, flowing rapidly without a ripple. Ambris reached out and put one arm round Ursulet and one round Morwen, but Lynett prevented him roughly.

"Not like that," she said. "The channel's narrow, and you must go in one by one, after me. Come now—blessed God, they're here—" and she flung herself into the water, pulling Ursulet by the hand after her. The lantern hit the water and went out, and the long howl of a hound broke out almost at their backs. Morwen and Ambris plunged quickly in.

It was surely like death. The shock, the dark, the cold—the bursting lungs, the rushing current sweeping away all sense of direction—as if asleep in a horrible dream, the eyes tight closed, nothing real but the frightful urgency to breathe—how could one count? . . . thirty-two, seventy-five, twenty-one, forty-four, oh, anything . . . and then somehow, his head was out of the water, and he was breathing, and thanking God for just breath—but the darkness was so total he might have been blind. He put a hand above his head and touched rock less than a foot above him, though he could feel solid ground under his feet. He felt a terrible fear of the roof closing down on him again—if he went in the wrong direction, he would get pushed into another horrible crack—oh, which way? And then above the rush of the water he heard Lynett's voice: "This way! This way! Keep over to your right—have no fear, the roof's high enough here—" and struggling in the direction of the voice, he found his knees scraping on the bottom where the water ended on a sandy beach, and cautiously he stood up. Still all was inky black, but he felt other bodies standing round him, and they clasped each other, dripping, shivering like wet dogs. They were all there, Lynett, Ambris, Ursulet, Morwen—and for a moment they clutched each other's bodies in the dark, indiscriminately, desperate for human contact and reassurance.

"A step or two more this way," said Lynett. "The water's behind you. Now you're safe. Now stand still, all of you, while I go and find some light."

She left them and they could hear her groping round.

"Can she see in the dark?" Morwen whispered.

"I suppose so," replied Ambris. "Indeed, I don't know what she can't do."

Lynett could be heard crunching over pebbles, shuffling, stumbling; then they heard the sound of flint on steel, and in a minute they saw a faint flicker of light glimmering out.

"Come over here, but carefully—the going's rough."

They groped towards the light. By its gleam they could see they were in a vast cavern—how big, the light was too faint to show them, but they seemed to be in a world of looming rock columns and arches, receding into endless echoing night. Underfoot the ground was rough and ankle-twisting—they made their way with difficulty to where Lynett was sitting crouched over the little glimmering torch she had managed to light. She had, they found, uncovered a cache of small pitch torches, with flint and steel, and a stone jar she was uncorking.

"Here's something to save our lives," she said, and poured each one a drink, in turn, from the stone jar—she had a little silver cup hanging from her girdle. It was a rich, sweet liquor, thick and creamy, and wonderfully heartening. "They call it King Arthur's Ambrosia," she chuckled. "The shepherds make it of eggs, and strong mead, and cream, and lemons, and they drink it when they go lambing in the snow. They say it will raise the dead, or make a barren woman conceive."

"You had all this prepared for us?" asked Ambris, with wonder.

"Oh, yes, my lad. I've been here before, a time or two, and I knew it would soon be needed. One has to look ahead."

"But how did you find the place?" (It was comforting and steadying to keep on talking.)

"Oh, a blind man brought me here once or twice. Long, long ago, that was. Blind as a bat, but like a bat he could feel his way in the dark better than with eyes—yes, and swim like a fish too. Oh, but that was years ago. Well, Mordred and his dogs can't reach us here, and I've no doubt he counts us dead. So far so good. Yes, and another blessing—these stinking rags of mine have had a good wash." She laughed again. They were all feeling the better for "King Arthur's Ambrosia," and a little light-headed with the sense of escape—although their clothes were drenching wet and their bodies battered.

"You're not too bad, girlie?" Lynett said to Ursulet, putting an arm round her shoulders. "You don't know who I am—I'm Ambris's great-aunt."

"Did ever a man have two such great-aunts?" said Ambris, laughing too.

"*Two* great-aunts? What do you mean?" said Lynett, rather sharply.

"You and Morgan."

"Morgan? Have you seen her again?"

"Why, yes, or dreamt of her. She came to me in the dungeon—"

"All right, lad. I've no doubt she put you to the test, but I've no doubt she'd little success with you. *I* know, even though I can't see your face. But we still have to beware of her. No matter. If you're rested we'd better go on. There's a trace of a path here. Follow me in single file, and hold on to each other. You, Morwen, take the bundle of torches, and Ambris take the bottle. Oh, and one other thing I hid here for you." She held up a sword and belt, which she fastened upon Ambris, and gave Morwen and Ursulet two useful sheath-knives. "A man feels better if he has a weapon—so does a woman for that matter. Myself I always have my dagger on me—Now let's march."

❧❦

SEVENTEEN

Encounter with a Sibyl

How far they trudged and struggled through pitch-black caverns, they never knew. It was a long, hard day's march, so far as they could think it to be a day. Several times Lynett halted them for a rest, and gave them another drink of "King Arthur's Ambrosia." But they rested very uneasily, for their garments were still drenched and clammy on them, and dried but slowly, being thick wool and leather—they weighed them down, and chilled them to the bone too. Ursulet had lost her cloak and hood—as for Lynett, her shapeless rags flapped and squelched as she walked.

At last, far off, they saw a faint gleam of light coming from fissures in the rock high above them—then more, till their way became clearly visible—it seemed as if they must be nearing the outlet of the cavern. Suddenly they halted, once again on the brink of a dark, wide, slowly flowing stream.

"Are we to go in the water again?" asked Ursulet, with a sigh, and yet with such an edge of resolution on her voice that Lynett laughed.

"And by the Mass, I believe she would if I gave the word! Look, you boys, do you realise that she's never whimpered once? She's Arthur's daughter sure enough—yes, and Guinevere's as well, for Guinevere had guts too—No, my pigeon," and she drew Ursulet to her, "no need to swim again. I'll have a boat for you this time."

She raised her voice, and sent a long "Halloo—oo—" echoing to the other side of the water. A high thin voice answered her from the other side, and a woman came into sight.

In the dim light she was a strange object, very tall and thin, naked to the waist; a skirt of patched goatskins swung round her narrow loins. Strings of crystal beads dangled round her neck, and copper bangles gleamed on her stick-like arms; her hair, dusty grey, bristled out from her head. Red-rimmed eyes peered from under shaggy grey eyebrows. She held a torch above her head.

"Hey there!" she hailed them. "Whose name do you come in?"

"The Radiant Brow," Lynett called back.

"Of nine kinds of fruit?"

"Of nine kinds of flowers."

"All's well, you can come over," piped the old woman. "I'll fasten the boat to the rope. Pull it over."

There was a rough arrangement of wheels and pulleys on the bank on the travellers' side, and Lynett turned a wheel; a rope went round the pulley-wheel, which presently pulled a boat across the dark water towards them; they all got in, and with Ambris and Morwen pulling on the rope, reached the far shore. As they disembarked, they could see a glow of firelight, and far beyond that, a glimpse of daylight.

"Welcome, cummer!" the strange old woman greeted Lynett. "Nay, I knew it was you, but I had to try you with the questions—there are many deceivers about. Welcome, and your folks too. But I warn you, I've no good news for you. The cat's at the mousehole. You'll not get out *that* way. This morning they all came pouring into the gorge, Mordred and all his fighting men, and they've pight their tents, and sat down like a besieging army round the mouth of my cave. I think *she's* with them, and *she* hears and smells out the very emmets in the hills. No, you'll not get out that way."

"Then what shall we do?"

"You'll do as the mouse does—bolt out by another hole. There's only one way now, and you know it."

"What, the long way?"

"Yes—I don't know another."

"Then we must take that way."

"So you must, if you can. The Old Cold One is still down there, did you know? He sleeps much, these days, and with luck he'll not wake when you pass."

"We must risk the Old Cold One," said Lynett, and Ambris wondered with dread what they meant.

"But come," the old crone said. "You'll rest and be refreshed before you start again. I've meat and drink, and what you'll need more—warmth and dryth."

They followed her round a screen of rocks. First they passed a kind of niche like a chapel, where lamps burned and garlands of wild flowers lay fading in front of a hideous stone figure, whether made by man or chance-formed out of the rock it would be hard to say—a figure something like a woman, with the breasts and other sexual parts grotesquely exaggerated. The old woman hailed it with a strange sign as she passed it. Next was a little cell, evidently the old woman's own dwelling; peering from the doorway the bright eyes of a fox and an owl looked out on them. And then came a large recess where blazed a lavish fire of logs on a hearth of white sand. As they stepped on to the sand a grateful warmth met them, such as their shivering bodies yearned for.

"Now," said Lynett briskly, "here's what we need. Strip off your clothes, every shred, and we'll dry them for you here, and warm you too."

As they hesitated, she went on, "Let's have no nicety about this. We're all as God made us, and we're soldiers on campaign and make no fuss for modesty. I'll not have you all dying of ague and fever and the lung-rot, which as-suredly you'll do otherwise. Come now—the girl can stand behind me here, and you boys face towards the wall over there. Now strip, I say."

They did so, she throwing off her clothes too; and the warmth of the fire and of the dry white sand was heavenly to their chilled bodies. The old woman ran round picking up their wet garments and hanging them over poles in the glare of the fire. Ambris kept his face turned to the wall, but the thought of Ursulet's slim white nakedness on the other side of Lynett fairly took his breath away.

❦ ❧

EIGHTEEN

The Cold-Drake

WARMLY clothed again, and adequately fed with roast meat and herbs by the old woman, they slept on the sand round the fire; waking once in the night to hear the old woman intoning some kind of chant before the stone image—a waft of incense came across to them, not the kind they ever smelled in church, but hinting of aniseed, valerian and pinewood. And when the light from the mouth of the cave indicated that it was morning, they broke their fast on rye bread and goats' milk, and started off again, back down into the darkness of the cavern. The witch, for she seemed to have no other name, gave them a lantern with a lighted candle, and to each one a long staff of ash, tipped with an iron spike, to help them in walking. So they went back into the dark, and Lynett picked out a way for them, not the same as that by which they had come.

"Tell us," said Ambris, "what is the name of the kind hostess of that place?"

"She has no name. They call her the Witch of the Hole, for all that the folks know of this place is a hole in the rocks. And yet I think she is not so much a witch as a priestess of the older gods. She and her forebears have always been there, mother to daughter, time out of mind."

"And how did you come to know her passwords?"

"Ask me no questions, boy. As I overheard you say, 'I don't know what she can't do.' There's much about me that you don't know."

And with that they trudged on in silence.

"What a strange smell," said Ursulet.

In a few minutes more the strange smell had become an overpowering stench. There was a horrible odour of decaying meat and animal filth, but besides that, the smell of some strange animal such as none of them had ever met before. At the same time a feeling of coldness, a freezing horror, began to creep over them.

"What is it?" cried Ambris. "What are we coming to?"

"The Old Cold One," said Lynett, lowering her voice.

"What in heaven's name *is* the Old Cold One, then?"

"A cold-drake."

None of them could help shuddering at the ominous word.

"The fire-drakes are all gone," Lynett said, "but here and there a few of the ancient cold-drakes live on. This one has been here for who knows how long—the simple folk outside worship him, and bring him offerings—sheep and cattle now, but once it was men. Sometimes he sleeps for months together in his den, and I'm hoping we may get past his den without waking him. Go quietly now."

But after about fifty yards more, Lynett halted with a sharp indrawing of breath, and motioned them all back with her staff.

Right in the narrow path where they stood, a thing like a treetrunk, or a black basalt column laid on its side, lay right across the way. It seemed to be made of stone, till one looked more closely. It was a neck—the body to which it belonged was hidden in the recesses of the rocks, but the head in which it ended lay on the ground, flat and blunt like a snake's, and measuring more than a fathom each way. A bunch of skin and quills on the back of the neck hinted at a crest, now folded; and the eyes were tight shut, the long eyelids lying in leathery folds. And from it came both the horrible smell and the feeling of a cold breath.

"Can we get past?" Ursulet whispered into Lynett's ear.

"I doubt it—I had hoped he'd be inside his cave."

"Look," said Ambris, and he too dropped his voice to a whisper, "I could cut his head off here—"

"Don't you try," retorted Lynett urgently. "You'd only bruise him and wake him in a fury. His skin's like horn."

"Could we step across him?" Ursulet suggested.

"One might get over, but not the rest."

"Then what are we to do?"

For once, Lynett seemed at the end of her resources—and as they hesitated, the creature's eyes opened in two long gleaming slits, and the head raised itself from the ground, and like a snake's began to weave to and fro, searching. Then its great body heaved itself out from its hole in the rocks, and it raised its head and its huge crest erect, and its eyes and mouth strained open wide—the eyes enormous, round and fiery-rimmed, the mouth full of teeth. The cold breath steamed from it like a fog. It came lumbering towards them, its head swinging.

With one impulse the four of them scattered and crushed themselves into crevices of the rocks, as the creature, clumsily gathering speed, crashed past them and down into the tunnel whence they had come. They heard its great footsteps shaking the earth as it receded.

"Come quickly now," cried Lynett. "It can't turn in that narrow passage-way." Together they ran forward, across the great trace left by the cold-drake's neck. And then they heard it again.

"Oh God—it's coming back!" cried Lynett.

"What can we do?"

"No use to run—"

"Is it vulnerable anywhere?" Ambris panted, tugging at his sword.

"Only the eyes and the mouth."

"Then this is what we do," said Ursulet. suddenly taking the lead. "This must be done together. We've our staves. Ambris and Lady Lynett, you've the longest reach—make for its eyes, one the right and the other the left. Morwen and I will thrust our staves into its mouth and try to hold it down. It's coming—"

And sure enough, in the dim light—for Lynett's lantern had gone—the beast came up again out of the depths, its ugly head seeming to float in mid-air before it, eyes round and glaring, mouth distended, a bluish light flicking around its dripping teeth. It made no sound but its harsh breathing and the thunder of its heavy hoofs.

It was upon them.

"Now!" cried Ursulet, and the four of them struck home together—Ursulet felt her staff catch and sink and wrench in her hand, as the cold-drake writhed and struggled— Morwen's staff held firm beside hers, and she felt them clash together—she ground hers down firmly, trying to ignore the poisonous teeth that grazed her wrists. She could not see what Ambris and Lynett were doing. But Ambris felt his sword thrust deep into the cold-drake's eye, and reach something soft. The cold-drake lashed and shook them, like a bear shaking dogs—and then its resistance slackened—its jaws clashed together and Ursulet and Morwen sprang back as the great teeth shore through the ash-staves, but it was its dying convulsion. The struggles ceased, and the repulsive head lay on the ground.

The four drew back, and leaned against the walls, shaken and faint. Lynett was the first to speak.

"Well done all. Champions all of you—and my Ursulet, she's a general. Cheer up, it's over now."

But Ursulet was convulsively crying, in Ambris's arms, her head pressed against his shoulder. Behind them Morwen, crouched on the ground, was shivering like one with the ague. Lynett put her arm round him.

"All's well, my boy. Yes, here's another one who is of the true blood of Arthur, whatever men say. Come, lad— Look, we must get away from here—the cold breath of the cold-drake still hangs about and daunts us. Come away, and leave the Old Cold One. He'll give you no more trouble. What! Heads up and look like victors—we've slain a dragon together."

She had no torch now, but the cavern was less dark than it had been—it was all pillars and sheets of clear crystal and alabaster, and from somewhere above, light, very faint, filtered down. As they gathered themselves to march again, Lynett said,

"I had always heard that the Old Cold One guarded something, but I have never known what it is."

How far they marched after it was hard to say—on and on, into the dim world of stalactites, sometimes darker, sometimes lighter. The terror of the fight with the cold-drake began to pass from them, and they walked on more hopefully, but as they went, more and more quietly, for the floor of the path where Lynett led them was no longer so rough—the uneven rock gave way to sand, white, soft and deep, so that their steps hardly made enough sound to wake the sensitive echoes of the glassy pendants above them. They felt afraid to speak even in a whisper. And then they found themselves passing through stately arches, which could almost have been made by human hands—arch after arch, and below them screens and curtains of hanging alabaster, till they stepped into a hall of solemnity and wonder.

A high vaulted roof extended above them, shaped by good mason-work—the ribs of the vaulting converging in a carved rose far overhead. A smell of incense floated there, holy incense and no witch's brew. Lamps hung on chains, burning quietly, and tall tapers on sconces, their flames burning without a flicker. And their light showed a circular space, as it were a chapter-house. Round it lay twenty-four couches, and on them twenty-two knights, all in their armour, laid with their feet to the centre. And in the centre, on a stately bed, was Arthur.

The knights lay, deep asleep but breathing. Their breath rose and fell like a scarcely heard music. Bare-headed they lay, but each one's helm was by his right side, and each one's hands were clasped on his breast, and his sword, sheathed, lay girt to his left side. Over each one's head a shield displayed his name. They were all there, the earliest ones of the Round Table—Sir Kay, Sir Griflet, Sir Tristram, Sir Gawain—yes, Lancelot was there, though that seemed strange to Ursulet, who had last seen him as a skeleton-wasted hermit. He lay there fresh-cheeked, smooth-haired, young.

There was one couch empty, awaiting its owner, and that was Sir Bedivere's. And Galahad was not there, for he was in a far holier place.

And Arthur lay golden-haired, golden-bearded and calm; and above him the shield proclaimed:

ARTURUS: REX OLIM: REX QUE FUTURUS

The four stood awestruck, and with one accord sank on their knees, and so remained for long minutes. Then Ursulet rose, and walking reverently, but as one who had a right to be there, approached the couch of Arthur, and the rest followed her.

At once a deep voice, coming as from nowhere, boomed out across the vault,

"Is it time?"

And all the knights stirred in their sleep, with a clink and hiss of metal as each one laid his hand upon his sword. Urgently and in a whisper Lynett made the response,

"No—no—no—not yet."

The whisper carried like a grey wave through the still air of the vault. The knights folded their hands back on their breasts. But Arthur had raised his head from the pillow, and his eyes, those unforgettable blue eyes, were open. Ursulet stepped up quickly to his right, and Lynett behind her. Lynett, with a gesture curiously practical in the strange place, picked up a cushion and propped his head with it. Ambris came up to his left, and Morwen behind him. So they waited, till the King's lips framed themselves slowly into speech, and his voice came halting and indistinct as from far away.

"It is not time—but there is a word I must speak."

He reached out his hand, groping—Ursulet took it in hers, and the cold of it sent a shock up her arm, but she held it, and tried to send the warmth of her own body pulsing down into the cold body of the King. He spoke again, gathering strength.

"Ursulet, my daughter—my little Bear. My crown is yours, but you will not rule in Britain. Not now. Not yet." He paused, and drew a sighing breath, then reached out his left hand towards Ambris on his other side, and placed Ambris's hand in Ursulet's.

"Ursulet, Ambrosius, I join you," he said. "Remember what I have done. For you must carry on the line of those that look for my returning."

He rested a moment, then spoke with more energy.

"Mark this. Men give their names to their sons, and the mother's name is forgotten. And if the line from father to son is broken, the name is lost. But the mother-line—ah, that runs on, hidden and forgotten, but always there. You, my child—to be the mother of those that believe in me. Thousands of them—millions of them—mother to daughter, without name or record. No Kings—but Queens a few, and commoners without number—here a soldier, there a poet, there a traveller in strange places, a priest, a sage—from their mothers they take it—some pass it to their daughters—"

"What, father?" she whispered, bending her face to his. "What do they take and pass?"

"The fire," he answered. "The fire that is Britain. The spark in the flint, the light in the crystal, the sword in the stone. Yours, and your children's."

His eyelids drooped, then opened again, and his look passed to Morwen, kneeling spellbound beside Ambris. He felt the blue eyes upon him, and the cry seemed to be forced from him.

"My lord—grandfather—have you no word for me?"

"Morwen," the words came slowly. "Morwen—" he seemed to brood on the name, and then a look of pain crossed his face. "Ah, pity, pity. I could have made a man of you. I could have made a knight of you. At least do not slay your brother."

The noble head shook and again the eyelids fell.

But once more he opened his eyes, and said loudly and clearly,

"I shall come again. Let Britain remember—I shall come again."

Then he fell back into deep sleep. Lynett withdrew the pillow and, like a nurse, laid his head back softly on the couch, and placed his hands on his breast as she would a dead man's—but this was not a dead man.

"Come away now," she whispered, but Ursulet knelt still by the couch, and laid her head on the sleeping arm of her father, and wept deeply. And so the others waited for her in silence at the door of the vault, till presently she joined them, pale, hands clasped, and with her eyes on the ground.

NINETEEN

Up and Out

THEY resumed their march, quiet and dazed with awe. The path was a little wider here, and now Ambris and Ursulet walked side by side as with wordless consent, and her hand was firmly clasped in his. No word had passed between them, but it seemed that everything had been said.

The strange glow that emanated from the Chapel of Arthur followed them, and lightened their road some way; then it faded from them and died, as the hanging, glittering alabaster gave way to rude rock, and the darkness shut down again. Lynett called a halt, lit another of the small pitch torches from the scrip she carried, and shared out a little food, the bread and cheese and ale that the Witch of the Hole had given them. Ambris came a little nearer to her in the dimness.

"Aunt Lynett," he said, speaking very softly, "tell me this only—who fills the lamps for Arthur?"

"I do not know, my lad," she replied. "There are some who know, but they may not speak."

"But are they—is the Chapel, and the assembly of Knights and all of it—are they in this world or another?"

"And that I do not know. I might guess, but if I knew I might not tell. One thing I may tell, though—I have no eyes to see the things of the other world, but I saw this. . . . But to say truth, I did not know that it was *here*. . . . I'd often heard tell, since he—went away, that he rested somewhere, with his chosen knights, till the time should come—but I never thought that I—that *we* should see the place."

"And—when will the time come?"

"God in his Wisdom knows. But not yet."

"Will it now be when—when his true heir is crowned?"

"God in His Wisdom knows."

97

As they went on, the path began to climb. Ambris gave his staff to Ursulet, for hers had been broken in the cold-drake's jaws.

"This is hard going," said Morwen, stumbling and recovering himself with a hand on the wall.

"Harder yet to come," Lynett threw back at him over her shoulder.

"Whither are we climbing, then?"

"To a high place."

"And—how do you know the way?"

"I have my waymarks. Now mind the path, or you'll fall." And she said no more.

There began to be rough steps, cut out of the night-black stone, where Lynett's torch sometimes picked up a faint scintilla of crystal. Then the steps were more than rough—sheer shelves, where they had to climb from shelf to shelf. At the same time the confining roof fell away—as far as they could see, hear or feel, they were no longer going along a tunnel, but ascending the side of a wide shaft. Behind them was a terrifying drop into blackness, whence a cold wind howled up and tore at their hair and clothing. Up, up to the point of exhaustion. Five times at least Lynett's torch blew out, and they had to wait while she worked its red ember back into flame. Each one of them kept their balance precariously—Ursulet with the help of Ambris's staff—and shuddered at the gulf behind.

It seemed as if they were climbing like flies up the side of a room, to where it joined the ceiling. As they squinted up past the light of Lynett's torch, they could see the black roof above their heads, and no way further on. But here Lynett stopped abruptly at a ledge that just allowed room to pass, and led Ursulet to the front.

"Now you must go first," she said, her voice coming back sibilantly from the roof. "You *must*. It is right that you should."

"But where? Where?" exclaimed Ursulet.

"Straight up."

"But—there's no *up*. It comes to an end."

"You *must* go up. Up to the roof, and press on the roof with your head and your hands."

Bewildered, Ursulet braced herself to obey—and then she saw, on the ultimate step above her, brightly luminous against the darkness, the shape of Morgan. Morgan was, as always, white-robed and golden-sandalled, but all over her seemed to be sharp points of ice, bristling outward like sword-blades.

"Go on," insisted Lynett.

"I—I can't. Look—there!"

"I see nothing. Go on," said Lynett.

"But she—but *she* is there!" and in that desperate moment Ursulet understood that Lynett indeed could not see the baleful vision—but she knew also that Ambris could.

"Ambris, help me!" she cried.

"I'm here," he answered, behind Lynett.

The white lady above smiled coldly.

"Come on up," she said. "Come here, and let me throw you down backwards." And the needles of ice changed into needles of fire.

"Go *on*, go *on*," urged Lynett. "There's nothing there. Go *on*."

Ambris, looking up, saw Ursulet, small, helpless but still not daunted, dark against the white figure of the dreadful Lady; and a recollection of his mother's lore came back to him.

With all the concentration of his mind he pictured a great white pentagram, drawn from the left hand upwards and with the single point upright, in the air in front of the Lady; and then he pictured a long sharp dart of light in his right hand, and with all his might he hurled it at her, through the centre of the pentagram. And Ursulet saw the gleaming, flaming figure of Morgan shake for a minute, as a reflection in water shakes; and bracing her staff behind her, she trod firmly on the step, placing her feet as if she would trample those white feet in their golden sandals, throwing her body forward against the whiteness and the flames. There was nothing there.

"Wrench upwards!" cried Lynett from the step below, and Ursulet thrust against that crushing black roof. It cracked and gave and crumbled—and Ursulet broke through into blazing light, colour, shouting voices and the shrilling of trumpets.

Hands were drawing her up the last step, out of the hole, into the air—faint and pale, dusty and dishevelled, she came up out of the ground, and saw the blue sky above her. She looked out through a tall stone archway, and people were all round her—solemn people in white, and gay people in colourful clothes and crowned with flowery garlands. Firm arms supported her, or she would have fallen. Trumpets blew, and a multitude of voices shouted,

"The Queen! The Queen! The Queen of May!"

Ursulet turned, amazed, to Lynett, who, with Ambris and Morwen behind her, was stepping out of the same strange well-like hole in the ground. Lynett smiled, and laid her strong hand on her shoulder.

"Have no fear, dear child. I've brought you where I wanted to bring you, thank God—to Glastonbury Tor on the holy May morning. Here are all your loyal people assembled to see you crowned Queen of May and Queen of Britain."

TWENTY

❦ ❧

Queen of Britain

QUIET, kind-handed women in long white robes led Ursulet away from the crowd through the back of the tower which stood on the Tor, into an encampment of pavilions, and there they bathed and anointed her, and combed her hair, and refreshed her with milk, honey and wine, and made her rest on a soft couch, while outside the chorus went on singing sweet songs about the Queen of May who had risen up out of the ground, like life out of death, like spring out of winter, to bring back the good times to her people. Some of them hailed her as Guinevere, Gwynhyfar, "the white one that rises up"—the white wave, or the white ghost.

Then they robed her in a dress of thinnest silk, all embroidered with the flowers of spring in every colour, and put a veil upon her head so light that it could have drifted away on the air but for the golden spangles that adorned it and the golden pins that fastened it. And on her neck and waist and wrists were garlands of the nine holy flowers—oak blossoms, primrose, corncockle, meadow sweet, broom, bean-flower, nettle-flower, chestnut and whitethorn; and on her feet were white slippers adorned with trefoils. And so they led her out to the people.

In the glare of the brilliant May sunshine, on the top of that high hill in the eye of the sun, the assembly awaited her, all faces upturned towards her. She looked round first for her friends, and found them near her, they too newly dressed as befitted the occasion—Lynett stately in black velvet, with a tall hennin where floated a scarf of scarlet; Morwen in blue, handsome as a prince's son should be; but what Ambris was wearing she could not have said, for she could only fix her eyes on his face. Next she noticed the stately men who stood around her—bishops and abbots in their robes, earls and knights, and strange men in white with hoods, who were not monks, and wore an unknown sign. And then there were the folk, the men and women and children, with garlands and nosegays and posies in their caps, and green branches in their hands, singing, singing for joy of May and its magic Queen.

Two solemn, richly-robed old men led her forward—one, they said, was the Bishop of Wells, and the other the Abbot of Glastonbury—and they said,

"Do you here agree to accept this, the Lady Ursula, daughter of Arthur the King, as lawful Queen of all the Britons and your liege lady?"

And even in that moment she noticed that they did not use the diminutive of her name, but called her the whole name: Ursula, the She-Bear herself.

And with one accord the crowd that packed the hillside shouted, "Ay!"

Then the two great ones of the church waited while Ambris—yes, Ambris—delivered into their hands a great crown of gold, lightly wrought and all interwoven with fresh spring flowers; and the Bishop and the Abbot together set it on her head; and all the people shouted again.

And then came an old man, bearded and in armour of a fashion of twenty years past—and she could hear surprised voices near her call him "Sir Bedivere." He carried his long sword before him, point upwards.

"People of Britain," he cried. "You all know that Arthur's own sword Caliburn went back into the Lake, whence it came. Now I, Bedivere, the last of the Round Table, bring you this sword to be the visible symbol to you of the sword of Arthur. Lay your hands on it, and swear to remember that Arthur is not dead, and that he will come again, and that till he comes you will keep faith with him and with his line."

There was a rush forward, as all within reach laid their hands on Bedivere's sword, now held by hilt and point between him and an old man in white, who was Melior of Amesbury; and those who could not touch the sword laid their hands on one another's shoulders, so as to touch those who touched it. But foremost among those that touched the sword, kneeling, was Ambris, and young Morwen close behind him.

And as Ursulet stood above them, the great crown of gold and of flowers on her head, and looked down from the great height of the Tor, with mile upon mile of green Britain swimming below her in the blue haze of the distance, she felt as if upheld on wings in the mid heaven.

✺ ✷

TWENTY-ONE

But Whose Bride?

URSULET slowly opened her eyes, and spread her limbs against the softness on which she lay. Sheets of fine white linen, a featherbed of the softest down—rich curtains, parted a little way in front, showed a window with coloured glass. For one heart-twisting moment she almost expected her mother to come in. For never since those far-off days had she known anything like this. Even in the good times at the convent, the life of a noble's child among the nuns of Wimborne had been austere on principle. But now as the guest, the royal guest, of the Abbot of Glastonbury, nothing was too good. And to come into it all so suddenly! She turned her face into the snowy pillow, and smiled as she remembered.

There had been a procession through the streets of Glastonbury, with crowds of people, thousands of people, shouting and cheering. The women and children threw flowers before her; but the most part of the crowd seemed to be armed men. They had escorted her to the Abbot's stately guest-house, and there had been a banquet, and so many important people had bowed to her and kissed her hand and made speeches, and there was talk that had flowed above her head, tired as she was. . . .

And then, somehow, she had found herself in a quiet moment in the Abbot's orchard, in the moonlight, under the full-blossoming apple-trees, and she was alone with Ambris.

There was so much he said to her, but certain things remained and would remain.

"You are my Lady and my Queen," he had whispered, on his knees before her. But she had drawn him to his feet again, and replied,

"I am your wife in the sight of God and King Arthur."

And holding both her hands he rejoined,

"Ah, but what am I in your own sight, my dear?"

And she had said,

"My true-love and my darling," and they had clasped each other in a long, sweet, blissful embrace.

She was recalled from her happy waking dream by the entry of the two pleasant pretty girls who had been given her for waiting-maids. They brought her a breakfast of the best frumenty, enriched with raisins and cream, and served in a silver bowl; and they hoped her Royal Ladyship had slept well. Royal Ladyship!—and such a short time ago she had been nothing but Urz'l, the Jutish farmer's drudge, whom he had sold for a cow. The maidens drew back curtains and opened the casements of coloured glass, and let in the light of a heavenly morning.

Then came Lynett, brisk in a dress of green linen with a white wimple and gorget.

"That's my little Queen," she said, and kissed her with clumsy gentleness. While the maidens brought washing-water sprinkled with sweet herbs, and dressed her in a white smock and a scarlet gown, and combed and braided her hair, Lynett talked, and explained some of the things that were still a mystery to Ursulet.

"Kingdoms must be fought for, alas," she said. "Your father, our great Arthur, held all one Britain from the Roman Wall to the Channel, and kept the Roman peace and the Christian religion there. But now all's divided, and the Saxons and Jutes and Danes crowd in upon us daily. Mordred sets himself up as King, and he now holds London and the East; but we have Constantine the Roman on our side, who reigns as King in York, and Cadwallo of the West, whom the Bishops uphold. And besides those we have Earls and Knights all over the country." She rattled a rosary that hung at her girdle. "Do you see this rosary? Look, the beads are made of acorns, and each acorn means a knight sworn to us with a hundred men, and each gold gaudy is an Earl—that's how I keep count of them, and nobody thinks I'm doing anything but saying my Paters and Aves!—Most of them are here, mustered upon this island of Avalon, or Glastonbury, or Ynys Witrin as they call it. Yet Mordred has his troops drawn out to encircle us between here and the place where we found you. He watched us as a cat watches for a mouse, and not a creature could pass between Wimborne and here—but I brought you by hidden ways, so that you rose up in the midst of Ynys Witrin, as we had promised them, Bedivere and I, on the first day of May. And now you are crowned Queen. It remains to hold your kingdom by force of arms, and secure it against Mordred and the Saxons. For he will even call in the Saxons to suit his own ends."

Ursulet shuddered.

"He wanted me to marry his son Morcar—but he tried to ravish me himself."

"I know. I was closer to you than you knew—And so we come, indeed, to the nub of the matter. All men will have it that a woman must have a man to rule for her, that a woman cannot rule alone or lead an army—God knows why not. And so they say you must take a husband. Now in proper times of peace, a woman has always someone to make the marriage for her—her father, or a guardian, who gives her in marriage. You have no one to give you in marriage—"

She paused, and Ursulet broke in quickly.

"But Arthur my father gave me in marriage to Ambris."

"Ha! I hoped you'd say that, though I might not put the words into your mouth. Bless you, child, and so he did. I was there—yes, it was no glamour. I can never see the sleights and visions conjured up by the Deceiver, or any of the people of the other world, but I saw that, and so you can be sure it was no delusion. But you yourself—in your heart, how do you regard young Ambris?"

Ursulet turned full to face her, regardless of the two maidens. There was no blush on her face, but complete simplicity as she answered, "I am his and he is mine."

Lynett clasped her by both shoulders and kissed her heartily; but at that moment there was a knock on the door. One of the maids ran hastily across and returned.

"Oh madam—oh your Royal Ladyship—it's the lay-brother to say the Lord Abbot awaits you below. The embassies have arrived. His lordship bids you make haste."

"Oh me!" sighed Lynett. "Now it begins—You must hurry down—but *remember*. . . ."

And she hurried out, while the maids put a robe of scarlet velvet over the scarlet gown, with facings of vair, and clasped a thin golden circlet round her head; then they led her out and down the staircase.

* * *

The Abbot's Parlour it was called, but it was almost as stately, if not quite as large, as a knight's hall; warmed by a big fire under a chimney, not under a hole in the middle, and hung all round with tapestries. Here the Abbot of Glastonbury, with the Bishop of Wells at his side, led Ursulet to the dais, and placed her in a chair of state. Further back against the tapestries she could see Ambris and Lynett but she could not see Morwen. The walls of the great room were lined with people—men, all of them.

Outside, suddenly a trumpet sounded, and there was the tramp of armed men marching in step and the rhythmic clash of armour. At a loud word of command it ceased as if cut off suddenly; then there was only the occasional faint scrape and rattle of metal that spoke of armed men standing still. The doors behind the screens were opened wide, and King Constantine the Roman entered, with a body of his guards, two and two behind him, moving as one—eight strong warriors, dressed and armed in the Roman manner, with square shields, short swords, and plumed helmets. But as each pair entered, they genuflected together to the crucifix that hung behind the dais.

Constantine the Roman, the third of that name in Britain, wore the tunic and toga of peace; he was a short dark man with a clean-cut profile and piercing dark eyes, perhaps about forty, self-confident and decisive.

He saluted Ursulet with great formality, addressing her as Ursula the daughter of Arthur, Queen of the Britons. He spoke in Latin, but Ursulet could recall enough of the convent Latin, now rapidly coming back to her, to understand. But the Abbot of Glastonbury replied in the Celtic language.

"Honoured lady and queen,"—and so on, through a long honorific preamble. Then, coming to the point.

"And so, honoured lady, it is apparent to all, that, for the consolidation of his realm and the better alliance with our friends and helpers the Romans, a happy and auspicious marriage should forthwith be arranged for you, our lady and queen. In these troubled times it is, alas, too evident that you have no kindred to stand as your sponsor, and give you in marriage; so, as senior cleric here, and as I claim, senior priest of all Britain and all Christendom—since here and nowhere else our Holy Faith was first preached—I therefore take upon myself the happy duty of being your guardian and sponsor. And as such, I am privileged to bestow your hand in marriage upon King Constantine the Roman, now reigning in York, and here present."

It was not until the Abbot had rounded off his resounding period that Ursulet found her voice.

"Oh, but no—no! I will not marry him!"

The whole company stood aghast—it was like a stone thrown into the smooth surface of a lake, shattering the reflections—A stone? A storm!

"Child, child, you mustn't say that!" fussed the Abbot in an agitated whisper. And the grave, fierce Roman bristled up like a cat.

"Quid dixit—nolet?"

"Nolet, domine."

The word he spat out, though Latin, was uncanonical.

Everyone's face was red, save only Lynett's and Ambris's. They were pale and tense, but approving. In the shocked silence, Ursulet spoke.

"I won't have it. You take me and give me, as if I were a possession to be bargained for. I'm not a thing, I'm a person—a Christian soul if you like, my Lord Abbot—"

"Yes, yes, my child, but you mustn't—you mustn't— Look, it's very important, don't you understand? We mustn't make the Roman lord angry—"

And he launched off into a long speech in Latin, too quick and complicated for Ursulet to follow—it seemed to soothe the Roman's feelings somewhat, for his hackles, so to speak, went down—his angry face relaxed a little, and he turned about, after a rather perfunctory reverence to Ursulet and the Abbot, and stalked out, his bodyguard clanking after him. The Abbot turned again to Ursulet. "I've told him you'll think it over," he said.

"Let *him* think as much as he likes," said Ursulet, "I'll think no different. I will not marry him. Now who is the next embassage?"

The next embassage was Cadwallo of Wales, with the Bishops of St. David's and St. Asaph's. Cadwallo brought with him an escort of only four rough shaggy-haired Celtic fighters—but two of them led with them young Morwen, round-eyed and frightened. He walked between them like a prisoner being led to execution; and he looked just what he was, an intimidated boy of fifteen, though obviously efforts had been made to make him look older. He was impressively dressed in the finery of a Celtic chief, with a heavy torque of beaten gold spreading across his chest, and a ceremonial golden helmet with horns. Ursulet looked across at him, wondering what he was doing there, and his brown eyes met hers with a desperate appeal she did not understand.

Cadwallo, thick-set and with brown tousled hair cut straight above his brow, made low and elaborate obeisance to Ursulet, and then motioned forward his harper, who had come in behind the little procession. The harper, a white-bearded, bald-headed man, bowed and sat down on a small stool placed for him by his page, who also handed him his great harp. He ran his fingers very sweetly over the strings, and then began a long laudatory ode, about the greatness of Britain, the resistance of Britain to the Romans (Constantine and his men being out of hearing) and to the Saxons; of King Arthur; of his beautiful daughter (Ursulet suppressed a smile)—of the union of the tribes of the West with those of the South, the North and the East, and their freedom for ever from the Saxon invaders. So far so good—and Ursulet, whose attention had certainly wandered a little with the sweet harp accompaniment, realised that the ode had come to its conclusion, and looked to see if she ought to applaud or praise the bard. But before she could do so, Cadwallo came quickly after the musician with his speech. This was long and flowery, and rather to the same effect.

"And so," he concluded, "having in mind the union of our peoples, under one strong head, or shall we say, two heads, one strong, one gracious, that shall henceforth be one—I come, my lord Abbot, to you as guardian of this lady. Were I not already married, you may imagine, I would gladly sue for her hand—but instead I would put forward in my place one of royal descent, to whom I have the honour to stand guardian—our young Prince Morwen, on whose behalf I beseech your lordship for the hand of the noble Queen Ursulet."

The Abbot, all nervous twitters, turned, hands clasped, to Ursulet. She, staring incredulous at Morwen, saw him shake his head and with his lips frame "no." A look of sheer agony was on his face.

"My lord Abbot," said Ursulet, "my answer again is no. I said no before, and I say no now. I will not be given to this one or that one."

Before the others could recover from this further rebuff, Morwen broke from his guard and knelt at Ursulet's feet, holding her hand.

"Oh sweet lady queen!" he cried. "They made me come here—it's not my wish at all. Believe me, I could not betray you, and Ambris, and King Arthur. Oh, I—honour and worship you, lady, but I'll not be made to marry you against your will. For I know you are already troth-plight to Sir Ambris."

The Abbot let his crozier fall to the ground with a clatter—the Bishop of Wells groped for the chair behind him and sat down. A wave of dismay swept through the room.

"Madam, is this true?" the Abbot gasped.

"Yes, it is true," answered Ursulet without faltering. Then quickly she glanced behind her, and spread her hands to draw forward Ambris, and Lynett, and Bedivere. They closed up around her.

The whole room buzzed with a storm of anger and frustration. Wherever she turned Ursulet could see nothing but angry faces, swaying to and fro, and hostile hands shaken towards her; everyone was shouting at once. Only Ambris's hand sought hers, and held it with a steady pressure. In her mind's eye she could see Arthur's calm pale face, and feel his hand laid across their handclasp; and a strange boldness inspired her. She raised her voice and spoke loudly across the noise.

"Listen, all of you. Arthur my father has joined my hand to the hand of Sir Ambrosius here, and from that act I will not yield or move. Tell that to Lord Cadwallo, and Constantine the Roman, and the Lord Mordred himself. I will not marry any other."

Cadwallo came shouldering up out of the crowd.

"Then, my lady Ursula, you cannot expect me to fight for you. I bid you farewell." He gestured to his men-at-arms, who held Morwen grimly by the shoulders and dragged him away like a condemned criminal. The Abbot of Glastonbury stood below the dais wringing his hands.

"Lady, lady—don't you understand? You can't do this, you've wrecked everything. Cadwallo will withdraw his army, the Roman has withdrawn his already. How will you win your kingdom from the Saxons?"

"By God's help and King Arthur's," said Ursulet, feeling uplifted on a tide of supernatural excitement. The Abbot shrugged his shoulders, shook his head, and turned away.

"May God help you then, lady," he said, "for you'll get little help from men."

And the turbulent crowd began to stream out of the far doors, leaving Ursulet and her three friends alone on the dais, the excitement slowly dying out of her and leaving her cold.

"Oh, I hope I did right!" she exclaimed.

❧❧

TWENTY-TWO

Counsel from the Enemy

INSIDE the precincts of Glastonbury Abbey, which was Avalon, was the holiest spot in Britain, the little church of wattle and clay that was the shrine of St. Joseph and of Our Blessed Lady; and from this, holiness radiated like the beams of the sun. The nimbus of glory permeated the Abbey Church beside it and the Abbey itself with all its demesnes—a great area of ground lay within a ring of consecration, where nothing ill could enter. Even down through the Abbot's orchard, on the side furthest from the town, was holy ground. But at the end of the orchard, beyond trees and shrubs, there was a fence of wrought iron, that marked the limit of the hallows.

Beyond that, the wild country came up to the boundary of the fence, and there the holy powers had no hold. The country around the Isle of Avalon was for the most part bare and open, wet and reedy and treeless save for a few willows, but here on the edge of the Abbey ground there was a wood, old and neglected, of alders and birches, fast falling into the swamp, dark and ominous. Here, in the red light of sunset, Ambris walked by the railings, with the trim orchard and the hallowed ground on his right hand, and the darkling wild wood on his left. And there suddenly, with a rustle of draperies, was Morgan, facing him on the other side of the fence.

This time she was not radiant in white and bejewelled, but clad in a subtle sombre grey that merged into the colours of the wood behind her; her dark hair was covered with a pearly-grey scarf, but round her neck could be seen a glimpse of strange bronze amulets. She spoke in a whisper.

"Hist there, nephew. . . ."

He turned upon her.

"Get thee behind me, sorceress! I know you now—I'll

not listen to you." And he turned to hasten away. But she spoke mildly.

"Now, now! Is that any way to greet kith and kind? Is it kinsmanly, is it kindly—is it any sort of family feeling? Should there be ill-will between near relatives, on both sides of the family? You ought to spare a word for your great-aunt."

He knew his danger, but could not break away from her. He turned and walked along the fence in the opposite direction; she turned also and walked with him, matching his pace, turning when he turned, as two dogs will run on opposite sides of a fence. Her feet rustled softly, lightly, on the dead leaves.

"I must not listen to you," he said. "I know you are the Deceiver."

"Oh, sweet nephew! Call me deceiver, call me evil, call me a devil in woman's form if you must—but don't disdain a warning, even if it seems to come from your enemy."

"Warning?" He frowned, alert to something new.

"Yes, warning. Dear trusting boy, you don't know what you're doing. You love this Lady Ursulet, do you not?"

"That is no concern of yours."

"Ah, no doubt—but believe me, in your love and devotion to her you are serving her very ill."

"What do you mean?"

"Ha, you'll listen to me now?—Why, yes, don't you understand? She has her kingdom to fight for, she needs all the help she can get—a woman in her position must have strong allies. She should marry so as to gain the help she needs. Now do you understand?"

His heart sank.

"But we love each other—"

"Oh, dear lad, beware of love! Queens may not marry for love as others do. Love has been the ruin of many kings and queens. Think of Guinevere and Lancelot. Will you ruin her for the sake of this love?"

"I tell you Arthur himself plighted our troth to one another in his cave. We are already lawfully wedded."

"Oh, my dear young man!" She laughed. "Have you not seen enough of visions and waking dreams to know that they can deceive you? I can call up all sorts of shows, as well you know—and so can others. Even your own mind, and hers, in that dim strange place and after all you had endured—you saw a vision? No doubt you did, but was it of any more reality that the sleights I could show you? But come—kingdoms can't be won with visions and illusions. How is she to lead an army? How is she to defeat the Saxons? And what if she has to face Mordred's army too, and Constantine's, and Cadwallo's? Who is to be her war general? You, dear child? Or old Bedivere, with his rusty armour? Or your crazy old aunt Lynett? Believe me, that old woman is as mad as a March hare, and thinks herself a war commander, riding about the country in her old leather jerkin—do you know, she is your Lady's worst enemy, leading her on with notions of military conquest. There is only one effective war leader in this land, and that is Constantine the Roman. And it is he that she must marry, and gain both a general and an army."

It came over Ambris like a cold wind that she spoke truth.

"What must I do then?"

"You? You must go away from her—now, at once, quietly and without farewell. Otherwise, as long as you are here, she will not marry another. If you love her, as you say you do, you must cease to stand in her way."

"It will break her heart—it will break mine too."

"What are broken hearts to kings and queens? If you stay with her, and force her to fight this battle alone, there will be many more broken hearts than hers and yours. Again I say, think of Guinevere."

He drew a long breath—oh, she was right, of course, and yet. . . .

"Listen," he said, "why must you compare me to Lancelot? We are free to wed lawfully—there is no bar between us—my love for her is pure and unselfish and without any self-interest—"

"Yes—is it so?" She halted in her pacing to and fro, and faced him through the coils of the wrought iron, with the dark wood behind her. "Altogether pure, and wanting nothing for yourself? Tainted with no base desire? Oh, my dear self-deceiving boy—look me in the eyes. You are a man as other men are, and her body is a woman's body of flesh and blood. Are you sure, are you so very sure, that you desire nothing for yourself?"

He raised his eyes to hers, and then his face slowly reddened, and he dropped his eyes again.

"You see," her soft voice went on, "your motives are not so pure after all. Can you in honour seek her for yourself, and ruin her? Come, if you have any noble regard for her—break away at once. No goodbyes—no chance to relent. Go anywhere, but go now. Be brave—it will hurt less. Go—go—"

"I'll go," he cried in a choking voice, flinging his arm up over his eyes; and he broke away from that enchanted corner, and ran through the gardens, now grown dark—not towards the Abbot's house, but towards the stables.

And the shadowy lady gave a deep sigh of satisfaction, and melted like a breath on a window pane.

❧ ❧

TWENTY-THREE

The New Round Table

THE maid at the door of Ursulet's room let Lynett in, but shrugged her shoulders, spread out her hands—The curtains of Ursulet's bed were still closed, though it was morning. Lynett flung them back, and disclosed Ursulet lying face down on the bed, abandoned to violent weeping. Hardly looking up, she thrust into Lynett's hand a small scroll of parchment, written in the laborious characters of one not very used to writing. Lynett read,

"Farewell, my love and my lady. It has been shown to me that I am a stumbling block in your way, and therefore I take my leave for pure love of you. Marry the Roman, for Britain's sake and your own. And I, if I live or die, it is for you."

Lynett stood tense, crushing the scroll between her hands, and swore—slowly, deliberately, and religiously.

"Oh, God's Blood!" she said, "oh, God's own Precious Blood—" It was almost more a prayer than an oath.

She paced to and fro for a moment, and then turned to the shaking figure on the bed.

"Look up, child—you know what this means?"

"It means he has forsaken me," came the smothered reply. "Oh, dear God, this is the end! Let me die. How could he, after my father had joined our hands?"

"Ay, how could he? Never of his own will. No, my girl, listen. This is the Deceiver's work. To think she should have got at him at the last—now! No, lift your head and stop crying. Do you want to please *her* by despairing? Come now—do you want a dash of cold water on your head? Well then—get up and wash your face."

She stamped to and fro, while the waiting maids brought water, and Ursulet suffered herself to be washed and dressed.

"But what do we do now?" Ursulet asked at last.

"We'll call a council of the earls. What the devil—we're not alone. We've men to call upon."

"Must I marry the Roman, then?"

"The Roman? God forbid! Nor either of the sons of Mordred. Poor Morwen, though—I fear it will go hard with him—No, my little Princess, you'll wait till our Ambris comes back, as come back he will. With an army, no doubt, to turn the scale against our enemies."

Like a nurse soothing a child with promises, she persuaded Ursulet, who at last came slowly pacing down the stairs to meet the council of the earls—pale-faced and great-eyed, now looking like the White Ghost indeed.

It seemed that the council was not to be held in the Abbot's great parlour, but elsewhere. Lynett led Ursulet out of the Abbot's house, and across the green acres where the apple-trees still shed their blossom, to the Abbey Church. It stood tall, though not as tall as it was later to become, when the world was to know it for a marvel. But already it was a stately house, towering over that which was much more holy, the little ancient church of wattle and clay.

On the south side, by the monks' graveyard, was a low doorway; and here they went in, and down a flight of steps. Ursulet shivered as they left the shadow of the garden and plunged down into the shadow of the chilly stone. The little winding staircase led her out into the wide crypt under the Abbey church, a dim vaulted place, lit only by small slit windows high up at the ground level above, and by torches set in sconces against the walls. These latter gave a red and flickering light, by which she could see a number of armed men, in the apparel of nobles, standing round the walls, and in the midst a great round table. It was covered by no cloth, but it was richly inlaid and blazoned with colours and gold; and in the midst was the device of a rose, from which radiating lines divided the circle into its proper "sieges"—twenty-four for the knights, the central one for the King, the Queen on his right and Merlin on his left, thus making up the magical three-times-nine.

Bedivere, approaching in the dimness, said, "Be seated, gracious lady," and Ursulet moved to take the Queen's seat, but Lynett urgently whispered, "No, not there," and firmly placed her in the King's own throne. Dazed, she sat down, and the others took their places all round the Table.

Melior the Druid took Merlin's seat on her left, but the consort's seat on her right was left vacant—with a pang of heart she realised why. Next beyond the empty chair was old Bedivere, the only face in the circle that she knew. A chair was placed for Lynett close behind Ursulet's throne, for only one woman could be in the circle.

One by one the knights stood up and, saluting with their swords, gave their names. Strange names that recalled those so often told in the stories of Arthur's knights, like them but not many the same—Sir Segwarion, Sir Mortimare, Sir Nondras, Sir Palarion—just a few were veterans from twenty years past, as Sir Ector and Sir Bors. Some were bright-eyed young men not yet out of their teens. The names went round in a hollow echoing ring, each with a grind of steel as the sword was drawn. Then when all were named, and Ursulet's eyes had wandered to the shadows in the dim vault above them, there was a clash of metal— each knight had laid down his steel-plated gauntlets on the table before him, and all joined their bare hands in a ring. Ursulet's hands were grasped by Melior on her left and Bedivere on her right, and behind her, Lynett laid her hand on her shoulder.

"Now listen all here," came Bedivere's deep grating voice, as rusty as his armour. "We here are the new Table Round, and the vows which our forerunners took at this Table, we take again, to live and die in faith and truth, to Arthur the King until he comes again, and to Arthur's heir, the lady Queen Ursula, the true Daughter of the Bear. To her we pledge our service and fealty."

And they all answered,

"We pledge our service and fealty."

Then Melior's musical voice broke in.

"Swear we all this. King Arthur is not dead. He sleeps, and will come again."

And the deep murmur echoed against the dark stone roof,

"King Arthur is not dead. He sleeps, and will come again."

Then all sat down, and for a time there was silence.

Presently, Bedivere looked up and said,

"But we are not complete. Where is Sir Ambrosius?" and all looked to Ursulet for an answer.

"My lords," she said, her voice coming cold and thin in that strange place, "he is not here. He—left a message to say that he was departing—that he would not—stay with me. . . ." She could not go on.

There was a stir, and a cry of "Treachery!"

"Where has he gone?"

"Has he betrayed us?"

"Has he gone to the enemy?"

Ursulet stood white and shaking, with no words to say. It was Lynett that came forward.

"My lords, may I speak?"

"Speak on, Lady Lynett."

"Then I'll say this, and say sooth—young Sir Ambris is no traitor. I'll answer for him with my head. He has gone, I know,—I'm sure of it as I'm sure that two and two make four—he has gone because he has been ensnared by the lady of deceits, the Enchantress Morgan le Fay. She knows how to turn a man's mind and make him think black is white—she has persuaded him that honour requires him to go and not to stay—oh, my lords, do we not know the power of her subtlety? Sooner or later he will return, but in the meantime we can do little without him. Our Queen is without her right arm. But oh, worthy and noble Knights, never call him traitor!"

There was a murmur of approval. Bedivere spoke for the rest.

"Be it so, lady—let the siege be left at our Queen's right hand for Sir Ambrosius, in trust that he will return. But now we must take counsel for the war."

There followed a long and wearisome debate, of which Ursulet could hardly follow one word in three. Maps were unrolled on the Round Table, and the knights pointed here and there—numbers of men, numbers of horses, distances from castle to castle, all flowed over her head. From her high throne she looked up to the murky roof, where the faint beams of light slanted down from the little narrow windows through the smoke of the torches. Oh, if only the Holy Grail could come slanting down along those beams, to put an end to all this round-and-round discussion and show them plainly what they ought to do!

For it seemed there was no agreement among them, no clear lead, no real plan. Too many plans were put forward, by too many with ends of their own to gain, and none would fall in with another's. They wandered into digression, quarrelled fiercely over side-issues. Bedivere tried to hold them together, but they swept him aside. As for Ursulet herself, she just could not follow the multitudinous arguments.

At last they adjourned for the noon-meal, and Ursulet walked out into the fresh air and bright sunshine on Lynett's arm.

"Oh, dear God," she exclaimed, "what are they supposed to be doing?"

"You may well ask," replied Lynett bitterly. "The fools —the fools. We haven't a leader. Not one leader among us. They will follow you, my dear, as a banner of war, but how can you know how to lead them? How can I? Oh, for a leader—"

"The Roman . . . ?" Ursulet faltered.

"No! *Not* the Roman—not at the price he wants."

"No—not at the price he wants."

The sunshine blazed on the apple-trees, but far to the north a thundercloud was building up. The air was oppressive.

There was a stir across the other side of the wide lawns, under the apple-trees.

"A messenger, lady."

A breathless man knelt before her.

"Lady—the Earl Mordred advances from the east, and is nearly at Winchester. He bids you yield, or he will shut you up here by siege. Constantine the Roman has declared defiance against you, and marches with all his army—he halted his homeward march at Reading, and the rest of his legions have joined him there from York. The Earl Cadwallo has proclaimed Morwen King in defiance of you, and holds Camelot."

Ursulet's face was as pale as the messenger's as they led him away.

"Oh God—what shall we do now? And Ambris not here—" She trembled on the edge of tears.

"No terror and no tears," rasped Lynett, "or I'll box your ears like a page, though you're Queen." Ursulet swallowed down her rising panic, glad of the harsh words. The livid cloud was drawing nearer, covering the sun. Not a breath moved. Far across the smooth lawns, she could see a small black cat, its fur on end, dancing madly in circles under the trees.

"One thing we'll not do," said Lynett. "We'll not stay

here to be shut in. To die of famine and disease, that's a filthy death. Let's break out of here while there's time, and face them in the field."

Melior, who stood close beside, stepped forward at the words. He was a tall, fresh-faced man, with serene blue eyes under his close white headdress. His voice, from which he took his name, was clear and sweet, the sweetest of any man's.

"One other thing, lady," he said. "None of these lords can agree, but there is one whom they will obey. Now is the time when we shall call upon Merlin himself to guide us."

"Merlin?" Ursulet felt her heart leap with unreasonable hope. "But Merlin sleeps in Broceliande, under the stone where Nimuë enchanted him."

"Not so, lady. I was the last to know Merlin. The Lady Nimuë was his faithful wife, and died before him, so always she waited and called to him from Broceliande, till his time came. I saw his passing, when he wrought his last wonder in the circle of Stonehenge—some day the story will be told. Merlin sleeps in the Otherworld, as many do— but I believe he will wake if we call him."

"Call him, then, oh, call him!—and if we may call him, why not—my father also? Is it not—Arthur's Time?"

"I do not think so, dear lady. Not unless Merlin himself, maybe, gives us the word. Arthur may only be wakened once again, and woe betide us all if he is waked untimely. I do not think it is the time. But Merlin will tell us."

"So be it. Let us call Merlin, for it may be that none other can help us now."

As they went down again into the crypt, the thunder had begun to growl in the heavy, sagging clouds. A strange tenseness plucked at Ursulet's nerves. She had noticed how, when Lynett ran a comb through her wiry grey hair before they rejoined the others, sparks crackled and blazed; even her own fine flaxen hair followed the comb as if pulled by it.

The crypt seemed very dark and oppressive. Little light came in through the high windows now; only the torches illuminated the stony space, red and fitful.

When all were seated in their proper places, Melior stood up. The golden Tribann gleamed on his forehead, and on his bosom the Snake-stone caught the flickering light, and seemed to glow from within.

Then entered two women, white-robed and bare-headed; one bore a bowl of water, and the other a smoking censer. Slowly and rhythmically they paced round the circle, sprinkling and censing, to cleanse and hallow it. The wreaths of smoke from the incense hung in the air in great solid swathes. Then Melior himself advanced, and placed in the centre of the Round Table a bronze bowl of ancient pattern, full of water. He resumed his place, and spoke steadily and quietly in his musical voice.

"Now let all earthly thoughts be laid aside. Let each of us look steadily at the bowl, filled with the water of the sacred spring—and with all the power of our minds, let us call upon Merlin to be here with us."

All fell silent, and in the silence the thunder could be heard, coming nearer. The sun, in its last brilliant glare before the storm, broke the clouds and for a second pierced dazzlingly down from the high window in the south; then it was gone again, and a black wing seemed to sweep over. A wind began to sigh in the rooftops and the treetops.

Still they all kept their eyes on the glimmering surface of the water on the bronze bowl; then Melior began chanting. Then he raised his voice and called loudly:

"Merlin! Merlin! Merlin-n-n-n. . . ."

And on the last syllable his voice hummed on and on and on, till they felt rather than heard it. And the smoke-wreaths that hung in the air above the Round Table moved together and grew thicker, and took shape. All saw it—a human shape, veiled and draped in the wreaths of smoke: "an old man covered with a mantle."

A voice spoke—slow, halting, as if not used to speech.

"Adsum . . . I am here. What do you ask?"

Melior was on his feet and leaning across the table.

"Speak in the Name of the One Above All. How is the Kingdom of Arthur to be won?"

Slowly came the words, and then faster and louder as the apparition gathered power.

"Not by battle, not by the sword. They that take the sword will perish by the sword. There will be no victory, no triumph of arms. The Kingdom of Arthur, like the kingdom of his Lord, is not of this world, else would his servants fight. . . . Not in this generation, nor for many to come, but generation after generation, soul after soul, mind after mind. . . . For the Saxons also will bow the knee to Arthur, but not now and not thus. The conquered shall lead the conqueror, and the vanquished shall overcome the victors. Shall the colours of the dyer strive against the cloth . . . ?"

"Oh, speak more plainly!" Melior cried. "Tell us—is it not yet Arthur's hour? Are we to wake him in this extremity?"

"No—no—no. Not yet. Not thus is it written. By Arthur's line, but not by Arthur's name. By blood, but not by bloodshed. By the distaff, not by the sword."

One of the knights cried out, "What, then—is there to be no victory? Are we not to fight?"

And another cried, "How do we know this is Merlin?"

"Be silent," said Melior, suddenly authoritative, and then addressed the cloudy presence.

"Are you—are you indeed my master Merlin? Give us a sign—"

"I am Merlin Ambrosius," the voice pronounced, and then suddenly changed from the hieratic to the tenderly familiar.

"Melior, you bad boy, you made the ass run away with my Plato."

The voice concluded with the dry chuckle of an old man.

Melior gave a sob as from the depths of his heart, and fell forward with his head on the table, his arms groping towards the feet of the apparition. Then he raised his head and looked round at the others.

"It is he—it is my old master. That was something none knew but he and I." Then he dropped his head again and they could hear him weeping bitterly. And again the thunder rolled above them.

The hieratic voice began again.

"Hail to the daughter of Arthur, Ursulet the Lesser Bear, daughter of Guinevere, bearer of the distaff. But where is Ambris? Where is Sir Ambrosius? Without him the prophecy cannot be fulfilled. Where is Ambrosius, son of Gawain, son of Gareth, son of Lot. . . ."

The voice was fading, and the figure began to dissolve—then the crash of thunder shook the roof above them, and the lightning fell. For a moment they all saw each other outlined in blue fire, and the shape of Merlin, not veiled now, but plain and recognizable, and in front of him, also plain to see, the shape of young Morwen, kneeling with his back to Merlin like a runner poised to start—he was naked and shining as if with rain. Merlin seemed to point with his hand and to release the kneeling figure like an arrow from a bow. Then the darkness closed down, and each one for a second seemed to be blinded. Melior's voice, intoning: "Thanks and blessing—depart in peace into the bliss of Gwynfyd," was all but drowned in the crash that followed the lightning.

They sat dazed and silent in the dark—the torches had blown out. Then, as pages ran to relight the torches, they gradually gathered their wits. The rain was roaring down on the high roof of the church above them, and at first it was hard to hear each other's voices. Ursulet had drawn Lynett to her, and sat trembling with her face pressed against Lynett's hard bosom.

Voices began to make themselves heard.

"What, so we are not to fight?"

"The wizard prophesied no victory?"

"Do you understand it?"

"No, do you?"

"This is no answer."

"This is no proper augury."

Ursulet suddenly felt strength and resolution come into her. She sat upright upon her throne again—then she stood and cried as clearly as she could,

"Worthy knights, hear me!"

But her voice failed in the hubbub.

Bedivere drew his sword and beat it against his shield, and the clamour pierced all other sounds.

"Silence for her Grace the Queen."

Now they were silent—only the rain hissed—and Ursulet said,

"Victory or not, my lords, we must break out of here. We must not be shut up in Avalon. Sir Ector and Sir Bors are my father's oldest veterans, with Sir Bedivere—I choose that they three shall direct the army. So let us go and prepare to march."

❦

TWENTY-FOUR

In the Lightning

T HE guards at Camelot, that great fortress within its circle of earthworks, where Cadwallo had taken the place that had long been Arthur's, had orders to wait upon the young Prince Morwen, protect him and watch him, but nothing had been said about restraining him. It had not occurred to Cadwallo that there would be any need to do so.

The storm that had long been creeping up on the countryside, sharpening everyone's nerves and weighing on everyone's brain, had broken in terrifying force—crash after crash, lightning flash after lightning flash, and the rain coming down in a hissing sheet through the solid dark that broke, every few heartbeats, to show all objects curiously reversed, white for black, before the dark came again. What hour of night it was, no one could tell. Some counted the flashes—others just hid their eyes and waited.

The two sentries in the passage outside the door of Prince Morwen's room had hidden the bright heads of their halberds, and leaned against the wall each side of the door, watching the flashes through the little arrow-slit that lighted the passage. In the pause between two roars of thunder the door creaked and opened. They turned and stared silently as into the lightning flash stepped a pale and luminous figure—Morwen quite naked, his eyes shut, his hands groping before him. His short brown hair stood straight out from his head in a wild bristling mop. Although he groped, he walked fast and surely as if someone were leading him. The guards stood spellbound and let him pass.

"Did you see?" the one whispered to the other. "Fast asleep, and walking—"

"Should we stop him?"

"We daren't. Stark naked, and walking in his sleep. The hand of God is on him."

"The hand of the gods is on him," said the other man, who believed in older things. "No, we daren't stop him."

Past sentry after sentry, it was the same. None dared lay hands on the naked boy who walked with his eyes shut in the midst of the thunder and lightning. Out into the pouring rain, with the levin-flash all round him—now the rain pouring over his head quenched his bristling hair, and his bare skin, washed all over, gleamed when the lightning flashed—but his eyes never opened and his feet never faltered. Down through all the long banks and winding slopes of the great fortress—at the foot of the long approach was the gatehouse, but the gatehouse keeper, seeing the pale figure pointing to the gate as a crashing bolt seemed to fall from the sky, hastened in panic to open, and let the terrifying ghost depart, and then ran to hide, leaving the gate swinging. What earthly foe could trouble them that night, when gods and ghosts were stalking the land?

Ambris never knew where or how far he had ridden after he left Glastonbury. Somewhere, maybe at Amesbury, after the morning broke, he had found himself tired out and thirsty, and had snatched a drink of ale at some tavern, and then later had found a corner of a field and slept. Later, waking dazed and dull, he had plodded on, without any plan. He had seen the clouds bank up and the storm grow, but had gone on through it in stolid indifference. Then when he had come out of his misery a little, and considered his situation, there seemed to be nothing to do but press on; for there he was in the middle of a very wet wood, with the light failing, and the rain coming down on him, and the thunder and lightning terrifying his unfortunate horse. Stopping still was no better than going on; so on he went.

Suddenly a flash of lightning lit up a figure standing right in his path—a naked boy, streaming with rain. His horse shied, screaming shrilly, rising with its hoofs above the strange figure—Ambris struggled and pulled on the reins, turning the horse, or its thrashing hoofs would have descended on the naked boy. He fought the horse round in a circle, and at last made it stand still, and quietened it.

Then he looked at the boy, who was leaning back against a tree, exhausted, and blinking his eyes as just awakening from sleep. To his astonishment, Ambris recognised Morwen.

In an instant he was off his horse and ran to catch Morwen, who collapsed into his arms. The boy was as wet as if he had come out of the sea, deadly cold and shaking. Ambris took off his cloak and wrapped it round him.

"Morwen! What in God's name are you doing here, like this?"

Morwen was frowning and blinking and shaking his head, and putting up his hand to push the wet hair out of his eyes.

"I was sent to you," he said, speaking rapidly as if not quite of his own will, "to say, go back to her at once, she needs you as never man was needed before, in Arthur's name go back to her, so says—so says—Merlin. . . ." His voice faltered and came to an end.

"Why, what's this, Morwen? Here, come awake. Drink this, it's as well I've a bottle at my belt. There—now pull yourself together. This is no night to go running about the woods as bare as an egg. What did you do it for?"

As he spoke, he held him close up against the flank of his horse, supporting him; under the thickest covert of a tree, he managed to find some little shelter from the rain. The thunder had begun to slacken off a bit, and the rain to decrease.

"I don't know," said Morwen. "Yes, I do—a man came to me—an old man covered with a mantle—and told me to get up at once, just as I was, and run, and run, and run to find you, and tell you—what I told you just now. So I had to. . . . But I didn't know I was dreaming—I was dreaming, wasn't I?"

"Yes, I think you were," said Ambris. "But it could have been a true dream. These things do happen. Tell me again what you had to say."

"I've forgotten it now, every word of it."

"Oh—that's a pity. But I think I remember it—was it that I had to go back—that Ursulet—that the Queen needed me? Was that it?"

"It might have been. I said it, and then it went from me."

"No matter—if I'm to go back—if I'm really needed,

and Merlin said so—he did, didn't he? Then I'll go back. Let's go."

"Wait a minute." Morwen was recovering his wits. "Look, we can do better than that. I know the men in Camelot Castle want to fight for Queen Ursulet. Cadwallo and the Bishops brought them here for that, no matter for whether she was to marry me or not . . . of course you don't believe I . . . oh, but never mind. The thing is, they will fight for her—*not* against her—if we get at them quickly and quietly. I am sure this is the road to Camelot— come back with me now, and we'll take them by surprise. The storm's passing, thank God, and the moon will give us some light. Old Cadwallo will still be in his drunken sleep, if we hurry. I've a plan—come on."

They rode on through the still dripping woods, Morwen riding behind Ambris, and they were approaching the outskirts of the forest, when the last flash of lightning suddenly showed Ambris the form of Morgan le Fay, standing full in his path, more radiantly beautiful than he had ever seen her. His horse reared up, for the second time that night, and he struggled to steady it, while Morwen cried out in sudden fear. The lightning passed, but a gleam like the levin played still around the white figure of Morgan.

"Go away from me!" Ambris cried. "Let me alone, witch-woman!"

"Who are you speaking to?" said Morwen over his shoulder, in a voice shaken with terror.

"To *her*—to *her*—don't you see her?"

Morwen saw nothing, but he felt the hair rise on his neck, and the sweat break out on his skin.

"Once more, go back!" said the beautiful terror. "You cannot win this battle, and that is no deceit."

"Leave me alone," Ambris retorted. "Woman, I know you for a deceiver. You nearly made a traitor of me. How long will you keep troubling me?"

"All your life, Ambris," she replied smiling. "For I am deeply rooted in yourself. All your life, unless—unless perhaps you will pay me to go away."

"To go away for ever?"

"Yes, for ever, if you will give me what I ask."

"And what is it you ask?"

"Your right hand, or—"

"Or—?"

"Yes, you have guessed it—your right hand, or your manhood."

"Oh God!" the cry burst from him. "Take my right hand, then."

"Agreed. I will send one to take it, and then you will know that I have left you forever."

"Be it so. But oh—" as the full agony of it swept over him, "I have a battle to fight—how shall I defend my lady without my right hand?"

She smiled that dreadful mocking smile.

"You could always choose the—other."

"God, no!"

"Well then—But never fear. I would not be so unchivalrous as to deprive a man of his right hand *before* a battle. . . . The bargain stands. Farewell for the last time."

Another flash of lightning wiped out the vision. Ambris's horse stirred and went forward again.

"Who did you speak to?" said Morwen. "I saw nobody."

"Don't speak of it," said Ambris, and they went on through the slowly clearing night.

The keeper of the gatehouse at Camelot had had frights enough for one night, so that when two men on one horse came clattering out of the darkness and bade him open in the name of King Arthur, and one of them named himself as the Prince Morwen, he let them through and asked himself the questions afterwards. At the citadel gate there was more explaining.

"I am the Prince Morwen. Rouse the next man of the watch, quickly and quietly. I need you to come out *now* to fight for the Lady Ursula and King Arthur's house." Word was passed from man to man. Some of them went softly, and made prisoners of Cadwallo and the two bishops. And as the dawn broke, silently and without noise of trumpets, a thousand men, one by one, had stolen away out of Camelot, and were heading southward towards the plains of Glastonbury, under the banners of Morwen, Prince of Britain, and Sir Ambrosius, the liege men of Queen Ursula.

❦

TWENTY-FIVE

Towards the Battle

"Of course, you ladies will stay here with the baggage-train when we attack," said Bedivere.

"Of course we'll not," said Lynett.

"But the safety of our Queen—"

"Not my safety, I note," Lynett said, smiling sourly. "No matter. By the Mass, do you think we'll be any safer sitting here in a ring of wagons, waiting for some rascally plunderer to set the place on fire?"

They had marched out of the Island of Glastonbury long before day, as soon as the thunderstorm had abated—the army of earls, twenty-four of whom were also Knights of the new Round Table; ten thousand soldiers, horse and foot, variously armed, followed by baggage-wagons and sumpters and camp-followers, a fantastic crowd. There had been no time for sleep. Ursulet, dazed and tired, had been made to stand high up on a wagon by the gate at Pomparles—the Pons Periculosus—surrounded by a rank of torches and banners, reviewing them as they went by. This was *her* army, she was told. And in a few hours they would be fighting for her.

After they had all gone by, she had been given a reasonably comfortable seat on the same wagon, and carried along in the midst of the army, with Melior, Bedivere and the two maids-in-waiting—these latter were quite frankly terrified, clinging to each other and crying. Lynett disappeared, and then presently came abreast of them riding one of her famous tall black horses and leading another. They rode a long way, to get clear of marsh country and narrow causeways, above all to avoid getting penned in a narrow place; but they went towards where they knew their enemy to be, not away.

After daybreak they halted, having come out into open country; the wagons were formed into a ring, and there they ate, and some of them slept for a short uneasy while. Now, under the cloth cover of Ursulet's wagon, they were gathered round her—Lynett, Bedivere and Melior. Farther off they could see where a very ancient chivalric pavilion, its bright colours faded, sheltered Sir Ector and Sir Bors, bending together over a map in a lantern's light. Smoke and drizzle drifted in on Ursulet, her head ached, and she felt the discomfort of having slept in thick heavy clothes. It was all rather grim and discouraging.

"Of course we'll be no safer here," Lynett pursued her theme. "You understand that, don't you?—And then again, the Queen must lead her troops into battle."

"No!" said Bedivere, and "No!" said Melior.

"But I say yes," said Lynett. "Arthur's daughter could do no less, and it's what she herself wants—isn't it?"

"Oh, yes," said Ursulet, but she felt her heart sinking. What she felt like saying was, "No, I don't want to fight at all—why didn't you let me stay in the Abbey?"—but she knew she must not say that. Of course she must want to fight. . . .

"I don't see why you men should keep all the fun for yourselves," said Lynett. "This is my fight, and the Lady Ursulet's too, and I wouldn't miss it for the world, nor would she—isn't that so, child?"

"Oh, yes," said Ursulet rather faintly.

"But ladies," said Bedivere, his leather corselet creaking as he turned with a courteous half-bow, "I think you hardly understand—has either of you ever been in a battle?"

"I have," said Lynett stoutly. "Heavens, man, you should know that. I was in all King Arthur's battles, all seven of them—I carried the King's messages, and brought drink to the fighters, and tended the wounded on the field—precious few there were to do it. Bedivere, you saw me yourself at Badon, unless you've forgotten—"

"Then you should know it's no place—"

"Rubbish! She's got guts for it, haven't you? Arthur's daughter—Besides, where else would she be safe?—Well then, that's settled. She will ride my other black horse—"

"I can't ride," said Ursulet.

"What—you can't *ride*?" Lynett's tone was completely incredulous. "You mean to say you can't *ride*?"

"No, I never learnt."

"Never learnt to *ride*?"

"No. Where would I learn to ride on a Jutish churl's farm?" Ursulet was beginning to feel more than a little resentment, now that they were no longer scrambling through dark passages, against this tough and masterful woman who was arranging everything for her.

"But you were in the convent before that," Lynett protested. "Didn't the nuns teach you *anything*?"

"Not riding. We didn't go outside the grounds—it was unsafe."

"Unsafe, fiddlesticks! Can't you remember riding before you went to the convent?"

"On a pillion behind a manservant—but the plain fact is that I can't ride, and there isn't much time for me to learn, and I'm not going to start now by going into a battle." She snapped her mouth shut. If she weakened at all, she felt, she might easily begin to cry.

"Well, then," said Lynett, "you must have a chariot. It's quite right for a Queen to lead her troops from a chariot—the great Boudicca did so. Have we any chariots?"

"We've one, I believe," said Bedivere rather dubiously.

"Right—order them to bring it here, and we'll have a look at it."

The chariot was brought—an old-fashioned affair, which had been kept more for show than for use, but it would work. It was lightly built, with two large wheels; it had a bench seat where the passenger and the driver could sit together, and a back rail, and was drawn by two stocky British ponies. There was a driver, a young man from the Western plains, who knew his ponies well. Forebears of his had driven chariots for the Romans before they went away.

"This will do," said Lynett. "You'll sit here beside the driver, where the knights and soldiers can all see you, and I'll ride close beside you and bear your standard. They shall see that Arthur's daughter is in the field."

"Yes," thought Ursulet to herself, "and Arthur's daughter isn't afraid. But I am, oh, ghastly afraid. But I have to go on in spite of it. And I will, too, only—oh, dear God, don't let me show it. When we faced the cold-drake in the tunnel, no one was able to see the way I looked—and I didn't have time to think about it first . . . and Ambris was there. But if Ambris has left me I might as well get killed —only it's going to be so messy and horrible. All very well for that Lynett—she's made of leather, heart and face and

131

all. But she's not going to see me look frightened. What the devil! She thinks I'm a queen, and I'll go on looking like a queen . . . only . . . oh God. . . ."

"What should I wear for the battle?" she said.

❦ ❧

TWENTY-SIX

The Hour of the Morrigan

AND so this was it, Ursulet said to herself—this was
the battle, that was coming nearer and nearer to
her every minute. This long line of little dark figures,
strung out before her, all shapes and sizes, but all bristling, dark against the sky. The two shaggy ponies, capably
controlled by the young driver, paced forward, dragging
the chariot that swayed and pitched so that she had to
brace herself hard against the back rail. She was wearing
a corselet, knee-length, of fine chain-mail, and a scarlet
cloak over it, quite distinctive and conspicuous; Lynett had
wanted her to wear her hair hanging loose, but she herself
had realised that it would be dangerous, and had it tightly
bound up behind her head with a red ribbon, and sur-
mounted by a little gold circlet. She had to be a sign and
portent to her followers, although she might also be rather
an easy target for her enemies. As she went along she did
her best to remember to shout—it was supposed to inspire
the men to follow her. Though she felt more like watching
in silent fascination how that line in front came nearer,
nearer, nearer.

Sir Bors and Sir Ector had to make the decisions as to
where to go and what to do. She had no idea about it, but
that this was the battle and they must go straight before
them. She had a dagger at her belt, which might do some
damage at a pinch, and a round targe on her left arm, an
awkward thing, but it might keep off some of the blows.
But they had not thought it right to give her a sword.

They were moving faster now—so were the enemy.
Gradually, gradually they speeded up the pace. Now, with
the rush of air, she began to feel better. Hoofs drummed
all round her, men began to yell, an infection of excitement
took them all—there was no point in being afraid of any-

thing anymore—one could just go, go, go—and then—*crash*!

It was the first blow on her shield—at the same time as the whole world broke up in a furious confusion of crashes all around her—she heard cries that seemed to be directed at her, and there were hands, hands, hands, clutching—the chariot rocked and swayed wildly, and then it was through the first rank, and both she and her driver were still there. Behind her she heard Lynett crying out, "Oh, well done!" But then there were men running in front of her, and another rank to break through. She realised that she had automatically put up her shield in front of her face, and was beating off the blows that rained randomly upon it. Then she looked past the shield, and the first thing she could see was a sword coming down on the thickness of a man's leg, like a cleaver on a butcher's block—but the blood doesn't flow like that from dead meat—this was spurting out like a red fountain. Another man, she couldn't tell if he were friend or enemy, was right in front of the chariot, his face the colour of clay and helplessly upturned —the chariot wheel went over him and on, and she felt the ribs crack under the wheel.

The horror of it made all seem unreal to her. It did not mean anything—these carcases being so horribly unmade right before her eyes, they were not people—not human beings, surely—just—things? And she, what was she doing there? Remembering for a moment what she had been told she must do, she uncovered her face, waved her shield, and cried, "Arthur for Britain! Arthur!"

Some quite unknown fighting man, below her, said, "But you're unarmed, lady," and handed her a sword. She took it—the hilt was still warm from the hand that had just dropped it—and somehow the feel of it in her hand made her feel stronger, more assured—she could do something now, not just dodge the blows. She swung it experimentally, and then thrust it full in the face of a fierce man who was bearing down on her. It met his cheek, and the blood flowed—then the man dropped and seemed to vanish. So she thrust again at the next one.

She could not tell how long they had been fighting. It was all a confusion, a struggling, snarling crowd. Then above her she saw two glittering figures, armed and mounted— Mordred and his son Morcar.

Morcar gave a loud laugh.

"Oh, look, father—here's my wife come to meet me in her chariot!"

Two of Mordred's foot-soldiers ran to the ponies and held their heads; they reared up, and the chariot rocked backwards, Ursulet clinging on and only just keeping her feet; and Morcar, with a quick movement, sent his short stabbing spear right through the body of the young driver.

Ursulet cried out, hardly knowing what she was saying,

"You brute, why did you do that? He was a *good* driver—"

"You won't need him now, my love," laughed Morcar.

Ursulet sprang quickly from the chariot to the ground; her foot-soldiers surrounded her at once, lifting their shields to cover her. There did not seem to be as many of them as there were, and when she looked round for her mounted knights, she could hardly see any. Somewhere she could hear the ponies scream.

Then through the surrounding ranks of the foot-soldiers she heard a frightening word passed from one to another.

"The Romans! The Romans are coming!"

And at the same moment there broke out the awful, terrifying sound of the great Roman war-trumpet—the Bull's Mouth.

They came cutting through the Britons like a knife through butter—the helmeted, red-cloaked men of Constantine, Britons trained like Romans, moving together at the word of command. Ursulet saw her men begin to waver and turn to run. Vainly she shouted to them: "Stand, stand! Forward, forward, for Arthur and Ursula!"

She could see Lynett, some way off, still on her towering black horse, swinging her sword, beating the fliers with the flat of it, scolding them like a fishwife, all to no avail.

Then behind her went up a new cry, "Ursula! Ursula! Arthur for Britain!" and other troops swept up from the rear, like the tide flowing into a river, and carried them forward again. A voice she knew said, "I'm here, my dearest—" and Ambris's arm went round her, and under his shield he kissed her.

Behind him young Morwen, with a thousand men from Camelot, swept in to turn the tide against Mordred; and even the troops of Constantine were checked by the sudden surprise, and broke their ordered ranks.

Ambris lifted Ursulet on to his horse before him; she held to him, but still her hand grasped the sword.

And in the midst of the confusion Morwen met with his father and his brother.

"God's death, you rebel!" thundered Mordred, charging down upon him, but Morcar was nearer in the crowd. Both the brothers had dismounted now, and were face to face.

"So, you milksop," said Morcar, "you've decided to try fighting for a change? No doubt because the women are fighting too. Come on—kill me if you can!"

He was within sword's length of him, and Morwen pointed his sword right at his breast—and dropped it again.

"No, Morcar, you know I can't kill you."

"Then I can kill you, you coward!" and Morcar whirled his sword high in the air, and brought it crashing down on Morwen's head. Ursulet saw it split the boy's head as one would break a plaster image, and she was too stunned to utter more than a choked cry. She saw Mordred laughing heartlessly as his elder son killed his younger son—and then from the towering black horse, Lynett's whirling sword struck down Morcar, and he fell over his brother. And Mordred gave a great cry that pierced through all the noise. "By a woman!" he cried, and put his mailed hands over his face, and swayed where he sat on his horse.

There rose before him a kind of mirror, a kind of screen, cutting him off from the sight and sound of the battle-field—and in that mirror he saw Morgan le Fay. But now her dress was blood-red, and dripping with blood; and the rich jewels that adorned her neck and girdle were all made of bones.

She laughed at him.

"Now you may call me the Morrigan," she said. "It is one of my names. And you, Mordred—my vassal in soul and body, you are coming with me."

"But my kingdom!" he cried. "Woman or spirit or whatever you are—you promised me the kingdom. But now my sons lie dead—"

"I promised you nothing. All I said was that I had power to grant your wishes—and then you pledged yourself to me as my vassal. You should have known better than to trust me."

He groaned, and could say nothing.

"And now—first I am going to send you to collect a certain pledge, and then, my vassal in this life and the life hereafter, you are coming with me."

The vision passed, and Mordred sat on his horse bemused in the midst of the battle.

In front of him was Ambris, with Ursulet on the crupper of his horse behind him. Ambris held his long keen sword before him, but he had no gauntlet on his right hand. Mordred whirled up his sword, and as Ambris parried upwards, Mordred brought the keen edge down hard across Ambris's wrist, and struck his hand clean off. A horrifying fountain of blood spurted up. But Ambris, whose left hand was close to Ursulet, snatched the dagger from her belt with his left hand, and as he fell forward, drove it with all his force into the neck joint of Mordred's armour, and Mordred crashed with him to the ground and lay still. Ursulet tumbled from the horse, avoiding its hoofs as it broke free, and knelt beside Ambris. The blood was still pumping from his arm. She looked round for Lynett to help her, but could not see her—so, with her every breath a sob, she quickly untied the ribbon from her hair, and tied it tightly round Ambris's severed wrist, to check that ghastly bleeding. Then she picked up the sword that had fallen from his hand, and stood over him.

Somewhere behind her she heard Lynett shrilling out,

"They break, they give! Mordred's slain—come on, come on, come on!"

But at that moment a more deadly rumour went through friend and foe alike—a rumour that turned to a cry, a shout, a shriek of terror,

"The Saxons! The Saxons!"

Like a landslide they came—hordes upon hordes, sheer weight of numbers overwhelming all before them. No poet chronicled that battle—who can chronicle a moving mountain? Useless now for the Britons to turn and unite against a common foe. Too late, exhausted and leaderless, they broke and were swept away—even Constantine's Roman army was scattered, and forgot the Roman drill—what use was it here? And so the dark came down.

In the last light of day, Ursulet stood on what had been a little hill, but was now a mound of dead bodies, with Ambris at her feet. She swung the long sword in a ring— she had beaten off the foes, one by one, and now she beat off the black crows that flapped nearer and nearer, and the foxes and the rats. There was nothing else to do, but to keep swinging that sword. Her red cloak was in rags and soaked with blood, her hair down over her shoulders, tangled and ash-coloured, but the gold circlet still clung crookedly over her brow as if in mockery. So the night found her.

❦ ❧

TWENTY-SEVEN

The Walkures

Two Saxons were crouching over a little fire under a thornbush, on the untidy, filthy field of battle, in the dark, when no man can fight. They looked up at the sound of plodding hoofs.

Two black horses, taller than any British or any Saxon horse, and a woman riding one, and a black-cloaked man leading the other. A tall thin woman it was, wearing a leather corselet—an old woman, with wild grey hair streaming out on the wind. She rode slowly, looking at each corpse as she came by it.

The Saxons cried out, and both pointed together.

"Look! the Chooser of the Slain!"

"The Walkure!"

"But they told us they were young and beautiful, and galloped fast along the sky—"

"How could they find their men if they galloped? And young and beautiful or not, this is the Walkure. Look at her face—"

"It's a god-touched face. Thor preserve us! May he send a younger one for me—"

Presently the Saxons, watching, saw the two tall black horses coming back, and this time each was ridden by a woman. The grey-haired one carried a man lying across her saddle-bow; but the other woman, sitting stiffly on her horse, and staring before her with eyes that did not see, was young, pale-faced and with streaming flaxen hair, a torn red mantle, and a golden crown, and the black-cowled man led her horse.

Both the Saxons shuddered, one made the sign of the Hammer of Thor; the other said, "The Lord between us and all harm!" and crossed himself; for he had once been a Christian of sorts.

The horses gathered speed in the darkness, and presently were heard going away into the distance. Surely there would be company in Valhalla that night.

❧ ❧

TWENTY-EIGHT

Rex Futurus

IT was a long while after that Ursulet opened her eyes to the light again. There had been a long, dark, dim time, when she seemed to have been carried in some way—she could faintly recall Lynett giving her a drink, and then only sleep again. But once she had seen Ambris's face through the mists, and heard his voice, so she was sure that all was well, and slept again.

But now she was full awake, though very weak and stiff and sore. She was in a little whitewashed bedroom, very neat and light, on a soft curtained bed, but in no place that she had seen before; and Lynett was with her, she also very neat, almost like a nun in a white gorget and wimple.

"What's this?" she said. "Where's Ambris?"

"You'll see him in a minute. Take it easy. Drink this."

"What place is this? How long have I been here? How long have I slept?"

"Why, one way and another, you've slept a good many days. I gave you a sleep-drink, or it would have gone hard with you—since the battle, and that's the best part of a week ago."

"The battle?" Ursulet struggled to rise. "What of the battle?"

"Ah, lie still. No more battles for us now. I'll tell you all that later. You're in a safe place here—this is the heart of the mountains of Gwent, where the Saxons will never follow us. This is to be your home—yours and Ambris's."

"Ambris! Oh, where is he? Let me see him—I won't rest till I see him."

"Here he is, then." Ambris stood by her bedside—pale, but smiling. His right arm was wrapped in linen and slung in a scarf round his neck, and he laid his left hand on Ursulet's hand.

"I'm here, my love, my princess. Yours in heart and

hand—but it will have to be my left hand now. I shan't wield a sword again."

"Oh, your hand! Your right hand! Oh, Ambris. . . ."

"My mother used to tell me," he said, "of an old heathen god who put his right hand in a wolf's mouth to save his people."

He smiled, and all round her the faces were smiling and cheerful—the room was full of sunlight and flowers— and yet there was something. . . .

"My mother's here too," said Ambris, as a handsome woman came to his side. Her eyes were green but soft-lighted, and her hair was white, but held a hint of redness.

"This is the Lady Vivian, come from Lyonesse," said Lynett. "She will live here now. They—fear the floods in Lyonesse."

Vivian stooped and kissed Ursulet, and Ursulet noticed how cold and tremulous her lips and her hands were.

Then they left Ambris with Ursulet for a little while, and they had a great deal to say.

Later, Lynett came and dressed Ursulet in a simple white dress, with a coronal of flowers; and in the little church on the mountain side, so small it might have been a hermitage, the solitary priest pronounced them man and wife— but Arthur had joined their hands long before.

Then they shared a quiet little feast together—the bride and bridegroom, Ambris's mother, and Lynett and Melior, in the kitchen of the farmhouse that was to be their home. A simple meal, and a cup or two of wine. And everyone tried to be light-hearted and happy, but something was amiss. And each time Ursulet asked questions about the battle, they shook their heads, or made excuse, or spoke of something else.

At last they had finished the meal, and drunk the wine, and said a seemly grace—and all drew their chairs in round the fire. Then Ursulet said,

"Now I must know the truth. Tell me about the battle."

And they looked from one to another.

Then Lynett said,

"Well, you'd best have it straight then. We're beaten, yes, beaten into the ground. The Saxons possess the land."

Ursulet gave a great cry, and bent her face down on her knees. But she said, her voice smothered by her hands,

"Go on. Tell me all."

"They swept us off the field by sheer numbers. Friend and foe alike—Mordred's men and even Constantine's Roman-trained legion. They made no odds who fought for whom—they fought for themselves. We were like sheep. . . ."

Ursulet wept quietly, and the old woman's voice broke as she went on.

"I should never have counselled fight. . . . Oh God, how should I know?"

"Never blame yourself," said Ambris, his arm round Ursulet.

"They have overspread the country, and hold Winchester now," Lynett went on. "Their king has set up his seat there."

"But Glastonbury?" Ursulet lifted her head. "They've not profaned the holy Avalon?"

"No—the approach through the swamps was too hard for them, and I think they feared the Tor—they think there is a devil there. So they went on to ravage the Baths of Sul, where they think the Romans have left buried treasure."

"And we—do we fight again?"

"We cannot. I doubt we could muster five hundred men. The Knights are gone—all slain—Sir Ector and Sir Bors, and our dear old Sir Bedivere—and many, many others—" Lynett's voice, husky with grief, faltered away, and she too hid her face.

"Why did you not let me die then?" exclaimed Ursulet, suddenly fierce. "Why did you not let us both die, with honour on the field?"

"Listen, child." The old woman had recovered command of her self and her old manner. "When I found you and knew how things stood, I had my dagger ready for you both, to give you the kind stroke and let you sleep—but Melior prevented me. He said he must save something more precious than Arthur's throne or Arthur's sword."

"Yes," broke in Melior's voice, "Arthur's true seed. That it is, which we must preserve. Merlin has stood by me in the night, through many nights, and I know what his meaning is. No power can stop the Saxons now—it is written that they are to possess the land."

"Oh God!" cried Ursulet. "So all is in vain?"

"No, not in vain. Like a plant that dies down in the winter, and guards its seed to grow again, so you two must raise the lineage from which all Arthur's true followers are to grow—not by a royal dynasty, but by spreading unknown and unnoticed, along the distaff line—mother to daughter, father to daughter, mother to son. Names and titles shall be lost, but the story and the spirit of Arthur shall not be lost. For Arthur is a spirit and Arthur is the land of Britain. And the time shall come when the Saxons, yes, the Saxons shall pay homage to Arthur too—yes, and other races we do not know yet. . . . But in the end, Cymry and Saxon, and others from over the sea, will all be one, and all will know the name of Arthur. And there will be those among them, like a thread in the tapestry, who are your descendants, many, many generations to come. Here, in your safe retreat in the mountains of Gwent, you shall be Arthur's Adam and Eve. So shall Arthur conquer, not by one war, nor by one kingship, that soon passes away, but by the carriers of the spirit that does not die. Not by any son of Arthur, born to take the sword and perish by the sword—but by the daughter of Arthur, born to give life to those that come after."

Ambris looked down at Ursulet, but her face was bent away from him.

"Arthur shall come again," she whispered, and he felt her tears fall upon his hand. Then she lifted her head, and looked up at him with new radiance in her eyes. "Oh, yes, yes—Arthur shall come again."